A Road up the Shimmering Blues

Sai Vittal Battula

Table of Contents

Chapter One

"Come on Viyon, over here!"

Viyon passed the ball across the court, stooping so low to prevent the ball from bouncing high and ultimately reducing the chances of it being 'stolen'. It was a trick he picked up at practice last week and has been practicing repeatedly since then to hone his skills, it came in handy now as he was being attacked by two power forward players of the other team.

Viyon Timothy Aleck, born May 29th to the Aleck's, an average American family of a registered nurse for a mom and a junior partner barrister in a law firm as a dad; you could say that they were comfortable. In between work and studying to pass the multiple examination that mom registered to write this year, she has little time to sit at home and bake cookies or Banana bread like other regular moms.

Viyon grew up being used to different babysitters coming around to tend to him every day after school when mom has to work a late-night shift. His has always been an organized life, mom made him a timetable that he adhered dutifully to Midday nap, lunch at 2 pm, at least two hours of study time every day, one hour for recreational activities and sports, dinner at 6 pm, and a lot of other things. Mom was like a coach except she was not always around and she didn't have a whistle.

Viyon's favorite babysitter was Shelley, a senior high school student at Mid-west high. She always found a way to bend mom's strict rules and induce some fun in their time together. Viyon has had a crush on her for as long as he could remember, he had confided in Jared his childhood friend who in turn encouraged him to own up to his feelings and let her know about it. He never told Jared about the outcome of his confession of love. It was too embarrassing to share. It was therefore totally unexpected when at the end of the summer break to resume a new school year, his freshman year at Mid-West Junior, Shelley had come over to the house to let him know that she was accepted at Cal-U (California University) and she would be leaving for California at the end of the week. They hung out that night playing video games, him trying as much to stop time and delay the inevitable while she gained closure on this stage of her life to move on to the next. That night before she left, she kissed him.

Viyon sat still staring into blank space long after she was gone. He felt like a thousand fireworks went off in his belly and exploded through his eyes. He was speechless for a good while. He found his tongue and ability to speak the next day when he recounted the tales of his encounter to Jared who imitated a mock version of Shelley swooning over Viyon.

"Kudos man! You got your first kiss."

Viyon wanted to deny that it was his first kiss but thought better of it, Jared could see through him without glasses and he had tons of questions to ask like: "does this mean we're boyfriend and girlfriend now?"

"Errrrr..., I don't think so. She's all the way in California and you do not have any contact info on her. Relax dude, we're the Casanova gang". Jared said with a wink while slapping his chest.

"What's Casanova?"

"I don't know; I saw it in a playboy magazine."

A flying ball hit him square in his face which sent him tumbling down to the court floor, out of his reverie and back to the present. The power forward on his team had attempted an overhead pass to him which hit him in the face because he had not been watching. The opponent stole the ball and traveled with it across the court, dribbling and dodging other players that attempted to steal the ball. Viyon blocked a shot from entering the basket which elicited a loud roar in the hall from the onlookers. His team rebounded quickly. Taking possession of the ball, he did an outlet pass, moving the ball to the shooting guard who did a slam dunk and scored the winning basket against the opposing team.

The hall erupted in a loud cheer as the referee blew the final whistle to mark the end of the game. Jared ran down the seat to the court, cheering for the team as he did. When he got to Viyon, he gave him their signature handshake and landed a punch on his belly.

"Ow!"

Jared shrugged; "You left yourself open. That was a good game man."

"Yeah!"

Jared followed the direction of Viyon's gaze to the spectator's stand and discovered why he sounded nothing close to excited about the game.

"Maybe she had to work late."

"Maybe." His mom had missed another of his games again. She had not given him any assurance that she would attend but he had been hoping that somehow, she would be able to make it for at least, half the time.

He was in his sophomore year at Mid-West Junior and he could count on one hand the number of times his mom has shown up for any of his games. His dad kept an unbroken record of never having attended at all. His attendance at parent-teacher meetings was a drag.

"Penny for your thoughts? Come on, let's go get ice-cream, maybe we'll find some girls there who want to take your number and have sex with you huh?"

"And what would you be doing?"

"I'll be enjoying the satisfaction that I get to make your life meaningful and rewarding on earth. I'm your sensei on all things, ladies."

"You haven't even had a girlfriend yet."

"My point exactly, one of us needs to hit that gold mine before we leave."

Viyon chuckled and slaps him on the back.

Jared leans in closer and whispers in his ear: "Bucky 2 o'clock, he's coming this way."

Their gym teacher got to them before Viyon had the chance to organize himself.

"Viyon Aleck!"

"Yes coach!"

"Good job today."

"Thank you, sir!"

"What was happening in court today?"

Viyon knew the coach was referring to the time when he got hit in the face by the ball but chose to act ignorant. Admitting to having an idea about what the coach was saying would mean something was wrong, and the last thing he wanted was to have a tete-a-tete with his gym teacher.

"What happened, sir?"

"You got hit in the face by a ball. Well, I guess it's a part of the game."

"Yes, it is sir, I guess so too."

Coach Bucky gave him an odd look, like I-see-what-you're-trying-to-do kind of face, before he said; "see you at practice tomorrow" and walked off.

Jared reappeared from the shadows after the coach left with a cheery look on his face.

"I found us the perfect place to get ice-cream, let's go."

"I can almost tell that I will regret this, this is a terrible plan."

"Hey! A little optimism Gandhi? Thanks."

"I'll see you in front in five minutes."

"Two… the clock is ticking."

Viyon got to the front of the school after a tiresome long walk down the corridor filled with sports enthusiasts who wanted to tell him how much of a good game it was out on the court today; even big Joe gave a nod in his direction when he passed. Viyon did a background check of the entire front yard of the school and came up short of Jared.

This dude was supposed to meet me out here, he thought.

"Pssst! Pssst!"

Viyon traced the strange sound to a disturbance in the bushes nearby, he heard a rustling sound just before that and figured whoever had the voice had to be behind the bush. He took a step closer and could make out the silhouette of the person behind the voice.

"Jared? Is that you?"

"Sssh... Don't say my name, get over here now, fast!" he whispered.

"What's your problem man? What are you doing hiding in the bush?"

Viyon didn't see the hand that reached out behind him and dragged him forward into the bush, clamping down on his mouth so that he did not scream or shout and draw attention to them.

"Calm down man, stop acting like a sissy, be quiet!"

"Jared?"

"Yeah..." he looked around nervously, making sure no one had heard his name being called, or him answering the name.

"Care to tell me why we're hiding in the bush like hoodlums when we should be out getting ice cream?"

"JARED! I GET YOU, YOU CAN'T HIDE FROM ME! I JUST WANT A HUG FROM VIYON, WE COULD SHARE?" the shrill, high pitched voice pierced the air just a couple of meters away from where Viyon and Jared were hiding.

"It's Sally," Jared whispered. "She's been chasing me around school all day."

"What does she want?"

Jared gave Viyon a fierce look that could be translated to mean - 'Have-you-lost-your-mind?'. "You heard her, she wants to share you. Maybe we could agree, she gets the waist down, I get the waist up. What do you think?"

Viyon would have burst out in uncontrollable laughter sorely because of the look on his friend's face; but all he wanted was a peaceful, fun, night out with his friend to celebrate his big win, and if Sally as much as gets wind of where they are, this night would be anything but peaceful. He was not about to spend the rest of the night with someone hovering about him, chipping away at nothing, so he kept his mouth shut and held back from laughing. They would definitely laugh about this later, he was sure of that.

The guys waited for a few more minutes before maneuvering their way through the bushes and out of the school gate. Convinced that they had put in a good distance between themselves and the school, and Sally alongside the school, they reduced their fast-paced escape walk to a trek.

"Phew…!" Viyon said. "That was close."

Both exchanged looks with each other, then burst out laughing. They laughed long and hard, each taking a turn to mimicry of what it was like hiding in the bush from a 'girl'.

"Alright star boy, we're almost there preparing to be dazzled."

Jared opened the door to a fast-food restaurant around the corner from the school.

"Hey I know this place, I've seen it a couple of times on my way to school," Viyon said.

"But you didn't know their food, did you? Prepare to meet the eighth wonder of the continent, MacTee's Ice-Cream."

"Uh-oh, this had better be good."

An hour later, Viyon was having his third cup of Ice cream, a gift from the pretty lady sitting two seats away from him. He had expected her to come over and start a conversation but she merely smiled at him and returned his 'Thank you' smile with a nod, then she looked away.

Jared was at a table a few feet away from Viyon, captivating his listeners with tales of his best friend's awesome traits, Viyon saw Jared get pecked on the cheek by one of his listeners and smiled to himself.

"It appears one of us might have a chance to hit that gold mine, sensei," he mused. Jared excused himself from the ladies and was at Viyon's table in remarkable time.

"Hey man, are you ready to go home? I just saw my dad's car round the corner. I got to get home before him, race you to it?"

"Arrggh, come on. I just started getting to know this pretty lady."

"That's great, where is she?" Jared looked around in an exaggerated manner trying to find the lady that Viyon was talking about.

"Never mind Jared, I guess she left."

"Hmm, I guess so too."

Both laughed and Viyon suddenly interrupted the moment with a challenge. "Race you to the house pretty boy."

"Hey!" Jared called out after him. "That was supposed to be my line. He took care of their ice cream bill and was soon running downtown with Viyon.

* * *

Viyon knew the moment he stepped into the compound that nobody was home. The lights were out and the place was as quiet as it could get on a school night when none of the parents were at home. If dad had been home, Viyon would have heard music blasting out of their home theatre the minute he got close by; mom would have had a meal cooking in the kitchen and all the lights would be on. The security lights never go off; Mom is more security-conscious than her husband who is a lawyer. Those two seem like two very unlikely peas in a pod and Viyon often finds himself wondering how they ever got to be together.

Viyon made his way gingerly across the yard to the front door, he has walked through this place a thousand times before and had the map of the house in his head. Running his hand along the wall; he located the light switch and flipped it, illuminating the sitting room. The light brought everything into perspective making the place look better. The voicemail machine had two messages from his mom telling him she'd not be home for dinner as she would be running a late-night shift. He played the next message after that was done playing.

"Hey honey, I'm terribly sorry about missing your game tonight. I followed up on it though, and heard you were amazing. I'm making it up to you, starting now... I had a pack of your favorite pizza delivered to the house. I'll see you early tomorrow morning. Love you darling!"

"At least there's pizza," he said.

He went to the kitchen where there was an opening where the pizza guy could slip it in and leave it and go. As soon as he turned on the light, he spotted the box of pizza right where he thought it would be.

"Aha!"

He grabbed a slice out of the box, nibbling on it as he put the rest of the box in the microwave to let it heat up a little. While he waited for the pizza to warm up, he rummaged the fridge for milk and apples. The microwave alarm went off and he stuffed both hands with pizza and milk; holding the apple in his mouth with his teeth as he made his way to the couch. Once there, he dropped his 'spoils of war' on the center table, making himself comfortable on the couch where he would spend the next couple of hours relishing his victorious conquest with the latest season of 'Mortal Combat'.

Being home alone sure had its perks on it. Had mom been at home, she would never have allowed him to litter the place with his personal items and settle into a box of pizza, while binge-watching a 'violent' movie. He chuckled as he looked around the sitting room and noticed just how much of a mess, he made in just a few minutes. He made a mental note to clean it up before his mom got off from work the next day. He loved his mom a lot and would not want her to be heartbroken, which is what she would be if she found the place in this state when she returned. His dad, however, was into a totally different case.

He heard movements outside the house and paused the movie to go and take a look at it.

"Who's there?"

"It's me, your non-existent lover," Jared said in an inflected voice.

"Shut up Jared, one of these days I'm gonna knock you down on your backside before you even get the chance to say who it is… Hey, who asked you to go to…! Don't touch my box of pizza…! Damn! That's mine."

Viyon finally caught up with Jared who had been running around the sitting room with the box of pizza in his hand; both reclined on the couch, having expended so much energy playing around. Viyon continued playing the movie and both guys watched, enthralled by the action happening in a plasma box in front of them until they passed out on the couch a few hours later.

Chapter Two

"Viyon, I was hoping I'd find you here," Jared said, slamming his locker shut before he sprinted off to Viyon's locker.

"Great! What is it like this time? Missed you at gym class today, what happened?"

"Err, well I sorta kinda had a stomach ache so I spent the time at the school's clinic."

Viyon eyed Jared knowing he was making up the story as he went. Jared hated P.E classes and always find a way to be spared torture every time. Viyon knew that already but they still had this kind of conversation every time after gym class, he made a mock concern face when he asked Jared how he was feeling.

"This would not happen to be that same recurrent stomach ache that happens only during the fifth period on Mondays is it?"

"Yeah, laugh all you want," he hits Viyon on the chest in a playful way. "Some of us are not sports deities like the rest of you and we carry ourselves with the dignity you know".

"We build muscles where it matters most," he points to his head. "Right here," Jared continued.

Viyon turned red trying to hold in his laughter and after a terribly long second, he burst out laughing. "I'm just saying, mom is a nurse, I could get her to run a check up on you."

"Yeah, thanks. Have her do that, along with the test that finds out how to make your best friend become dumb."

"Alright I'll drop it," Viyon said still reeling with laughter.

"Not a problem at all. I'm sure you'd like to find out what it feels like to have to communicate your thoughts with telepathy. Or sign language. Or drawings. You know, you could be playing charades for the rest of your life. That should be fun."

Viyon pretended to throw a punch at him which he dodged, moving quickly. And that spurred another minute of laughter from Viyon. Recovering quickly, Jared tackled Viyon and both arms wrestled their way out of the school's hallway, slapping the other's hand away like two ladies involved in a silly fight.

"Alright! Alright! You win," Viyon pulled away "because I let you," he added with a grin. "So, were saying?"

"What was that? What was I saying?"

"You were going to tell me something in the locker room earlier."

"I'm getting an afterschool job?"

"You're kidding right?"

"I'm eighty percent serious and that counts for a lot."

"How are you going to do that?" Viyon asked still trying to take in the spontaneity with which Jared came to this decision.

"Stay close and learn a few things. I told ya, brainpower," he said clicking his hand on the side of his head. "That is if you want to come with me, to get the job. I think you should if you ask me."

"I endure your face enough for 12 hours already as it is, I don't need to add even a second to that; but since you asked nicely, I will get the Job with you."

Viyon looked at his side to find that Jared was already halfway across the street and was now making his way into a restaurant just down the road.

"Jared! Wait up!" he slung his backpack across his shoulders, running down the road so that he could catch up with Jared.

Viyon caught with to him inside the restaurant, panting as he dropped his bags on an empty table closest to the door. A waiter came over to ask if they needed anything and Viyon requested a glass of water. Jared requested a meeting with the manager, after a series of hand gestures and head nodding, Jared pointed to where Viyon sat at the table with a glass of water. The manager signaled for him to join them and a few minutes later they were given the job. That is after the manager had drilled them on a couple of

Do's and Don'ts and had them answer some Yes-No questions.

The manager offered them hamburgers on the house and the duo were soon on their way back to their houses.

"That was cool man, way to put some of those your brain muscles to use."

"You can pay your tributes now," Jared said.

"And… the moment is ruined."

Jared waved at a blond lady in khaki shorts and tank tops at a shop across the street.

"Who's that?"

"She stays in the house three blocks from ours, they moved in a month ago."

"Oh… someone's got sparkles in his eyes."

"Yeah, I'm bidding my time. I'm gonna bring her in close as a friend then… BAM! I'll go in for the kill," Jared winked at Viyon.

"Err, I'm not sure '*kill*' is the word?" Viyon sights the lady coming over and informs Jared.

"Hey man, neighbor chick approaching at 2 o'clock."

"What?" Jared went into frantic mode almost immediately. "How do I look? Do you have gum? Give me gum, give me gum! Here, how's my breath?" Jared leaned close to him and breathed on him, so he could smell his breath.

"Hi…"

"Hi… Hey… Hello!"

"This is my friend Viyon, Viyon meet…"

"Cindy."

"Oh yeah, Cindy!"

Viyon shook hands with Cindy, "Nice to meet you!"

Jared came close to both of them and pulled Viyon off to one side, "Sorry man but you gotta go, I'll see you later. Don't try and get anything started without me, now Go! Go! Go!"

"I wonder whatever happened to, I'll bid my time and go in for the kill."

"That is exactly what I'm doing," Jared whispered. "Now go and stop being a pest."

Viyon made to leave but stopped and turned to say goodbye to Cindy, from the corner of his mouth, Jared whispered "You're trying to ruin my plans here man" and Viyon skittered off, hoping in his heart that his dearest friend doesn't do anything stupid to terminate his chances with her.

* * *

Miriam Aleck entered the house tired and exhausted; she had just finished a weekend call at the hospital and wanted nothing more than to soak in a bathtub and have a nice long hot bath. She dumped her bag on the center table and made her way up the stairs to the bedroom. Justin was sprawled across the bed snoring loudly which was not unusual for him, except for the lingering smell of weed. Miriam got out of her scrubs and walked into the bathroom naked where she turned on the tap so that it would fill up in the bathtub. The water ran for a while and stopped, she returned to the bathroom to find the bathtub nowhere close to being filled and tried to turn on the tap again but the knob won't budge, after struggling with the tap she finally realized what had happened: Justin did not renew their water bill.

She muttered a foul four-letter word as she stormed out of the bathroom into their bedroom. *Is it too much to ask for a necessary luxury like hot water?* The sight of Justin lying comfortably on the bed as though he had not care in the world only served to infuriate her more and she screamed at him.

"GODDAMMIT, JUSTIN WAKE UP!"

Justin rolled over and continued with his nap like he hadn't heard her, Miriam bent over him and yanked the blanket out from under him, that got his attention. Justin sat up, staring at her with bloodshot eyes made dull and dreary from sleep.

"You had better have a good enough reason for waking up like that?"

"The hell I do. You couldn't even pay the water bill? Is that too much to ask, Justin?"

Justin blinked his eyes at her and ran his hand over his face like he was trying to hold on to concentration and see her clearly. He shook his head and leaned back on the bed, using a pillow to support his head.

"Oh, the water's out?"

"You're damn right it is…"

"I had a few hitches on my way to sort that out but I'll have it done by the end of the week."

Miriam exploded then, pouring out all the pent-up anger. "I'm ashamed of you Justin, and you should be ashamed of yourself."

"Watch your tongue woman or I'll rip it out."

"Yeah, that's right! What else would you expect from a coward but to hide behind his strength? You know Justin I've just about had it with you, you've got a home: You've got a family, a wife, a son and you still act so immature and irresponsible."

"Miriam, I don't have the time for this right now."

"Oh yeah? Let's see when you have time? Hmmm… I know, NEVER!"

"Now you're just whining like a cute little kitten."

"I'll rather be a kitten than a man-child don't you think?"

"What did you just say to me?"

"I called you a child, a baby! Because you're no more than that to me. A man, a real man, knows how to treat a lady and take care of his home. You're no man, you're just a child."

Miriam turned to get out of the room but she had hardly taken two steps when the first punch hit her square in the back and she staggered, leaning on the dresser for support.

"Is that man enough for you now?" Justin asked.

He raised his hand to go in for a second hit but his hand stopped midair.

"Dad! Knock it out!"

Viyon had entered the house during the course of their argument and stayed close to the door to listen to them, he suspected that his dad would resort to physical brutality to drive his point home and he wanted to be close enough to stop him when that happens.

"Honey, you're back," Miriam drew him in and kissed his cheek. "Go get out of your school clothes, don't worry about me, I'll be fine. I'll be down to make dinner in a bit."

"I'm not leaving you here alone with him."

"Get your sorry asses out of my room, I'll like to go back to sleep if you don't mind."

"Let's get out of here Ma."

"Go ahead, I'll be down shortly, I need to make a call."

Mom made a call and they had water running in the house before she came back downstairs, Viyon was feeling restless and needed to work off the extra energy so he doesn't do something stupid so he changed into a sports jersey, picked up his basketball, and went downstairs to the kitchen.

"I want to do some practice mum; I'll be back in time for dinner."

Chapter Two

The look on mum's face said she understood the real reason Viyon wanted to leave the house so she just nodded her head and gave a sad smile. She watched him leave through the window in the kitchen, her eyes followed him out into the night as far as the light would allow until he disappeared from sight. Justin did not make any other sound since they left the room, so she assumed he had probably gone back to sleep. Her assumption was right.

* * *

Viyon bounced the ball around all the way to the mini basketball court down the street. Their house was close to the park where the basketball court is located and the neighborhood has enjoyed top security over the past years which was the sole reason mum would ever think of letting him out of the house so close to dusk.

Viyon believed he was grown up and could take care of himself but you'd have to tell his mum. When asked if she wanted another child, mum had said no that would rather pour out all of her love on him. As cute as it sounded, it came with an unwanted side attraction of mum's superpower, 'overprotectiveness', if that's an actual word.

Thinking about his mum reminded Viyon of the reason he decided to leave the house in the first place and he tried to distract himself by looking around the town and enjoying its beauty at night. The street lights were on, casting a golden look on the road as he walked. He spotted a couple on a bench at the park making out, and Jared came to mind. He thought about texting him but decided against it. Jared would sense at once that something was wrong and he did not want to bother him with his issues. He laughed at himself, if Jared could hear his thoughts right now, he'd be in big trouble.

Viyon got to the court and found it-empty, not that he had been expecting anybody but still he hoped to find someone when he got there. He did a few bounces and dribbling passes before he practiced his throw. After a few minutes of frustrating training, he gave up and bounced the ball so high it hit him back in the face.

"Aaaarrrrrggghhhhh!!!" he screamed, smashing his head on the ball over and over again. He knew his mom would see the bruises on his forehead when he gets back but he was past caring, he poured out all the pent-up anger, oblivious to the stares that were directed his way until he was done and he felt better. He picked up the ball and walked out towards the park's exit. He was ready to have dinner now. He could sit through the unpleasant company of his dad and be strong for his mum. He just hoped that this would not become a routine.

* * *

The next morning, Viyon got up early and was ready for school before his mum was done with her morning routine, which was very unusual. Jared came by and they walked down to the bus station to catch a bus to school together.

"Hey man, how are you doing? I thought you were going to stop by the house yesterday so I can give you some info on Cindy," Jared said, winking his eye as he said that last part.

Judging from Jared's countenance this morning, Viyon could tell it went well but he decided to ask anyway. "Uhn uhn! I'm guessing it went well."

"I got my way; I'll be ready to go in for the kill by the end of the week."

"That fast huh? plus we're still going to kill? Seriously dude?"

"Hey, hey! No time for details now, I'll tell you later. I'm not going to let you dampen my atmosphere, but I heard Bucky's going to be waiting for us in class when we get there."

"Oh-Oh! The midterm results are out..."

"That's right they are..."

"Shit!"

"You know, I still do not understand how you get nervous every time results are about to be announced, you literally freak out and you end up topping the class. I'm as calm as ice and I flop worse than anyone."

Jared paused as if in thought then his face suddenly lit up, "Maybe that's it. Maybe that's the secret, you get nervous and nature comes to the rescue granting you a wonderful grade, and 'Voila', you're the star student again. I'm gonna do it. I'm gonna get so nervous, your nerves will not be able to compare with my nerves."

Viyon covered his mouth with his hands to try and suppress his laughter. Jared does silly things like this but sometimes it's hard to tell when he is being silly or when he is actually serious and now it is one of such times.

"Pal, I'm sure that's not how it works."

"Yeah… say that and try to distract me but you're not getting my mind off target. Now, if I can just find something to make me get nervous…"

"You're going to have to continue that search inside the class because we're here."

The bus pulled up in front of the school prompting the student to file out into the school in their numbers. Sully faced Trevor spotted Jared amongst the crowd and called out a snide comment.

"Hey, douche bag! Results are out today. I wonder if you can flop worse than you did last term; but then again, I wouldn't put it past you to surprise us all, huh?" he looked at his sidekick for support, then laughed at his own joke and walked away.

"Don't listen to him man, let's go."

Coach Bucky entered the class five minutes later and called the class to order. After everyone was seated, he started handing out the scripts, from the corner of his eyes Viyon could see Jared still trying to get nervous. Bucky got to his table and handed him his script then moved on to the rest of the class. Jared let out a gasp when he got his script which warranted a snicker from Trevor and his goons.

Viyon refused to open his script, slipping it under the table instead. Mr. Bucky called him forward after he had distributed the scripts out to everyone and commended him before the class. Trevor said something and tried to cover it with a cough which Bucky ignored and continued with his speech, the bell rang to announce the first-period saving Viyon and the whole class from Bucky's speech. Jared made a face at Viyon as he went back to his seat, eliciting a chuckle from him. Viyon figured his friend would give him the full details of what that meant after class, for now, he concentrated on getting through the class periods before the break. The class applauded him on his way back to his seat, based on Bucky's instruction.

Jared waylaid Viyon on the way out of class to the cafeteria, Trevor was a few feet away from him, and from the look on his face, he did not look too happy to have been bested again in class.

"Hey man, what happened back there?"

"What do you mean?" Viyon asked looking confused.

"Hmm, really? Hold on a sec let me walk you through it," Jared scrunched up his face in a funny way "Erm... Bucky called you out in front of the whole freaking class man! You must have done a number on him. What was your grade?"

Viyon looked like he had been caught plotting a heist "I haven't had a look at it."

"You know; I feel like you do not appreciate the things that you have. I know for certain that if I have half the things that you have; I certainly would not waste it."

He walked away towards the cafeteria leaving Viyon behind where he stood to try to understand what happened to warrant such a reaction from Jared. Jared has always accused Viyon of not being grateful enough for what he has, but Viyon never knew how much he meant it or how serious he was when he said such. He took out the test script from inside his pocket where he had disposed it in class; there was an A+ written boldly in red on the front page. He scrunched it up in his hand and trashed it in the trash can on the way to the cafeteria, this was no different from the others he had before.

Chapter Three

Jared returns home from school and finds a Mercedes GLA 220 parked outside the house close to his dad's old jeep. He approached the house skeptically, all he could think of as an explanation was that his uncle Ron came for a visit. Uncle Ron was Jared's favorite uncle when he was younger but they grew apart as he grew older. He moved closer to the door and tried to make out the conversations going on inside the house, loud laughter and chatters are major indicators of uncle Ron's presence. He went in through the backdoor so he could escape upstairs to his room quietly but was intercepted by his mom going into the kitchen to get water.

"Honey, you're home!"

"Hello mom," he exchanged kisses on the cheek with his mom. "I was going to get changed before coming downstairs to say hi to Uncle Ron."

"Ron?" Mom looked confused. "Honey, Ron's not here but if you want, I could call him and let him know you miss him and you want to see him."

"No! No! No! No!" mom gave him a perplexed look. "Err… I mean… No don't call him, because I'm already doing that, right now."

"Oh! Okay, that's fine. Don't tell him about your dad's promotion, give your dad a chance to break it to him, himself."

"Dad got promoted? That's great news!"

"It sure is; it comes with an official car and a few other perks. He's in the sitting you should go say your congrats. Dinner will be ready in ten minutes."

Jared raced up the stairs to his room, got changed, and was back downstairs in time to set the table for dinner. He congratulated dad on the job promotion, conveniently leaving out the fact that the results came in today and his grades were no better than the last time.

"So, dad, theoretically speaking, let's say I wanted to run some grocery errand or maybe just do general day to day…"

"Yes Jared, you can have an old jeep…"

"Yes…! Thank you so much, you won't…"

"As long as you pay for the gas and you take care of your car repairs."

"Done! Done! Done! You got it. If you don't mind Mr. and Mrs. Rowland, I'd like to go show off my new vehicle to Viyon. See ya!"

"Jared, be careful!" Mom called out after him as he left.

He muffled something unintelligible on his way, stopping to grab the keys by the console on his way out. He learned how to drive last summer as a reward for staying afloat enough to get through to the next class, his dad had promised him then that he would handle over the jeep to him when he gets a new car.

Jared pulled out of the driveway into the street, he could just imagine the look on Viyon's face when he pulled up in front of his house. They had not spoken to each other since he saw him outside the class earlier at school.

Viyon was outside helping his mom take in the groceries she bought when he got there. He could see Viyon squinting to see who it was behind the wheels in the car; he knew the moment Viyon realized it was him as his face lit up and was immediately replaced with a questioning look.

"Duuuuuude!!!"

"Hey man, check out my new ride that was formerly my dad's ride but he got a new one so his old ride is now my new ride; so, it's old, but it's new," he winked.

"I got it, dude. It is so cool! MOM, JARED'S GOT A CAR!"

"THAT'S GREAT HONEY, PLEASE HELP ME BRING IN THE LETTUCE BEFORE YOU BOTH RUNOFF TO WHEREVER," Miriam screamed back at him from inside the kitchen.

Jared helped Viyon carry the rest of the grocery bags inside and used it as a chance to say hello to Viyon's mom before he yanks him out of the house for a spin in the new ride.

"Hi, Mrs. Aleck!"

"Hello Son, how are you? Heard you got a new ride huh? You guys are careful and come back in time for dinner. You're welcome to join us for dinner."

"I wouldn't miss it, ma'am."

Miriam smiled at him, while Jared gave her a peck on the cheek before they left the kitchen.

"Wait for it…" Viyon said.

"For what?"

"This…" Viyon mouthed a countdown, using his hand to represent the numbers when his mom's voice carried all the way out to the front.

"Do not forget to use the seat belt and drive within the speed limit. I'm not about to have my son in the ER for the weekend."

"Yup! Now we can hit the road, that's the last safety precaution for today at least."

Jared laughed and tossed the key over to Viyon, "You get the first 10 miles."

"Nope, I'll pass."

Jared looked perplexed wondering why Viyon would turn down such an offer until it slowly dawned on him. "You never learned how to drive."

"No, I did not."

"But I thought your dad promised to teach…"

"Let's not bring up my old man, shall we? Guy's a sad excuse for a father."

"I'm sorry man."

"Hey, don't ruin the moment. Now let's get this baby on the road. Whoo hoo!"

"Did you hear that?"

Jared paused in his step, inclining his ears toward the house to try and identify the origin of the sound that he heard earlier on.

"What is it, man… Oh crap."

Viyon could make out his parent's voices arguing inside the house, it took every ounce of self-control for him not to run back inside the house and punch his dad repeatedly in the guts until he passes out. Now he understood why his mom had not given him any trouble about leaving the house with Jared; she was so quick to consent and as excited as he was, he hardly noticed. The shouting continued, growing louder at some point and occasionally interrupted with threats from his dad.

The look on Jared's face made Viyon wish the earth would open up and gulp him up. Jared seemed terrified and lost for words, and Jared was never at a loss for words. From his reaction, Viyon could tell that this was a rare occurrence with the Rowlands and that served to infuriate him more. He was embarrassed by both parents so he asked Jared to drive him off somewhere far from here.

"I'm sorry man…"

"Let's get out of here and pretend we did not just witness that."

"Okay, got it" Jared tried to start up conversations in the car but after several listless monosyllabic replies from Viyon he gave up.

Viyon sat still in silence throughout the ride, staring out the window. He was so occupied with his own thoughts that he did not realize where Jared was taking them until Jared announced "We're here!" and pulled up in a parking spot.

"What do you mean here?"

"Trevor was talking about a party happening here earlier on this morning before I met you in the hallway," he turned off the ignition and turned to face Viyon. "You needed to get away and if I had told you where we were going you wouldn't want to go."

He saw a group of guys hanging out by the pool and his eyes lit up with excitement, "Whoo-hoo! Where the ladies at?" he screamed, then caught himself after he had gone ahead and noticed Viyon was still seated in the car.

"Come on man. This is it! This is your chance to unwind and let off some steam, you don't want to end up like Bucky," he leaned close and whispered. "A virgin at 50," then he winked.

Viyon laughed then unbuckled his seat belt and came out of the car, having completed his mission, Jared disappeared into the crowd with a bow to him.

"Guys check it out, it's the jock nerd…"

"Knock it off Trevor, why are you acting so thirsty for attention?"

Trevor turned sully and signaled the guys with him to leave, while they were walking away Trevor leaned close to Viyon and sneered at him.

"Let's get out of here guys, nothing interesting to see."

Jared surfaced a minute later with two cups of cocktails then handed one to Viyon shouting at the top of his voice so Viyon could hear what he was saying.

"Guess who I just saw?"

"Is this drink spiked?"

"It's a party who cares?"

"You'd be saying something different when my mom grounds me for the rest of the school year."

A song came up on the speakers and the crowd went wild, Jared along with them; jumping and singing discordantly along with the song.

"Whoo-hoo! Loosen up man," he was dancing and jumping now.

Viyon took a few sips of the drink and soon enough he was jumping and screaming at the top of his voice too. Jared excused himself shortly after, when he spotted Cindy at the pool with some of the guys from his class, leaving Viyon alone to handle himself.

"Viyooooooooooooooooooooooooon!"

Viyon turned to see Sally making her way through the crowd to get to him, he swore under his breath putting up a forced smile for her benefit. Sally navigated through the crowd and was beside him in no time. She was standing so close to him that he could smell every single item that had gone into her mouth.

"Viyon..." she breathed on his face. "Have you been avoiding me?"

Viyon moved back slightly, seeking to put as much space as possible between himself and the avalanche of bad breath that Sally was emitting; not one to take a hint or maybe she wanted to make him pay for avoiding her the last time in school by making him suffocate from lack of air, as he was holding his breath, she leaned in closer.

"Huh? Viyoooooooooon," she slurred her words. "You seem to be so scarce these days."

Viyon scanned the crowd in the party for a familiar face to come to help him out when he sighted Jared and Cindy at the veranda, the music was too loud and he knew there was no way he could scream at him for help all the way there from where he stood.

"I'm sorry please excuse me," he slipped away and called Jared on phone, looking at him where he sat so he could send him an eye signal should he turn to face him.

Come on, come on! Pick it up!

Jared finally got the call; from the corner of his eyes, Viyon could see Sally advancing towards him and he became frantic, he ducked behind a girl from class peeping through her sides to keep track of Sally's movement. Viyon lost track of her while still trying to get Jared on phone.

"Hey man, a little help?"

"What?!" Jared shouted. "DUDE YOU GOT TO SPEAK UP!"

Viyon swore under his breath before repeating himself to Jared, this time, however, he was louder.

"Man, I really need your help right now. I'm in the hall to your left, please man."

Jared turned in his seat to scan the hall, he had the phone in one hand against his ears while he swept the room in search of Viyon. He spotted him on the dance floor looking like he was hiding. Jared wondered why until he saw Sally closing in on him from behind, and Viyon did not have the slightest idea that she was close. As if by some telepathic communication, Viyon turned just as she reached her hands out to touch him, his face pleaded with Jared to come to get him fast as Sally locked arms with him and pulled him away.

Jared excused himself immediately and went in search of the mismatched couple. He found them at the car park with Sally looking radiant and excited without care in the world. Viyon however looked like he would book a therapy session with a shrink for a whole month.

"Hey Viyon, your mom is on the phone, she wants to speak with you," Jared said for lack of a better excuse.

"Why would your mom want to speak with you?" Sally asked.

"Well I don't know but I'll like to find out. Now if you excuse me, I got to go talk with 'my mom' on phone," Viyon disappeared out of sight, flanked closely by Jared. After they were sure that they had put a good distance between themselves and Sally, the guys took a seat and allowed themselves to laugh at the situation, after which Viyon requested that they go back home.

"I say we head back home now."

"Awwwwww man! Now's when all the fun stuff is happening."

"Yeah, but we're an hour and thirty minutes late for dinner."

"Oh shit! But you got to admit that it was fun?"

Viyon gave Jared a side look and asked; "What part of it, that last part was terrible."

"Yeah! It wasn't that bad though" Both guys laughed, remembering their late-night rendezvous.

Jared gave Viyon a few driving lessons on the way home, helping him out along the way until they came to stop in front of the Rowlands house. Both guys exchanged hugs and Jared went inside while Viyon jogged a little distance back home.

The lights were out in the sitting room and the kitchen but Viyon could tell that his mom was still awake, the fluorescent lights in her room were on. He imagined she was probably bent over another huge textbook trying to decipher the intricate makeup of the human anatomy. Moving through the side of the house, he climbed up the tree beside his window and let himself into his room. He had performed this act several times before it came to him naturally now. He usually leaves his room window open for this reason.

Miriam heard the quiet rustling of leaves and knew that Viyon was back. Her thoughts were confirmed when she heard his window slide open. She had stayed up waiting for him and now contemplated going to his room to get him to eat dinner or just talk but decided against it. She knew he heard them arguing before he left with Jared earlier that evening. She was concerned about him but decided that she would give him all the time and space he needed to work things out in his head.

She waited for an hour before going into his room to take him into bed and kiss his forehead. "I love your son"; she said, caressing his forehead before she stood up, turned off his bedside light, and left the room.

In the dark, Viyon turned in his bed, his eyes wide open, and whispered: "I love you too mom". He knew she was going to come and he had been waiting for her. Now he snuggled under the blanket and drifted off to sleep.

Chapter Four

"You ready pal?"

"Come on get it, let's go…"

"I mean because you've only had one lesson and I can't let anything happen to this bad girl right here," Jared said, tapping the hood of the jeep.

"That's why you would be sitting next to me throughout the ride, now get in or we're going to be late, 'Howdy boy'!"

Jared's face turned red with embarrassment: "You can never call me that amongst people," Viyon was trying so hard to keep a straight face and belie just how much he was enjoying this humor but his face betrayed him and he broke out in a burst of loud laughter.

"Yeah, yeah… laugh all you want. Now, let's go."

Jared was embarrassed by a childhood nickname that stuck. His mother called him 'Howdy boy', a much-preferred variation of 'Howdy-bunny' while he was growing up. He had loved it when it had started, it seemed kind of cute to him and he had answered to the name with pride, but the older Jared grew, the more he realized that he was outgrowing his 'cute little pet name', his mom, however, didn't think anything of it and occasionally still addressed him by the name despite his constant pleas for her not to. She had called him that morning when informing him that Viyon was waiting for him downstairs.

"It's not such a bad name. You used to love it once."

"Yeah, when I was five and shared bathroom with girls."

Viyon could not tell which was funnier, the expression on Jared's face as he said what he said, or the imagery that the words built up in his head.

"Hold tight, we're hitting the road in three… two… one!"

Viyon pushed down hard on the pedal causing the car to jerk forward and stop, he tried a few more times and the car started. The ride to school was a long and bumpy one with Jared yelling down instructions at Viyon while he maneuvers his way between other cars and people on the street.

Jared heaved a long sigh of relief when Viyon pulled up in the school's parking lot. The entrance into the school was anything but graceful and had some of the students gathered in small groups talking about Viyon's terrible driving skill or so Jared thought until they were in the hallway and a guy called out to Viyon.

"Nice drift man."

"Yeah," Viyon smiled back, a surefire message to Jared that he had no idea what he was being complimented about.

"Touché! Anybody noticed the car? Or me sitting in it? I was there you know, sitting this close," he gestured with his hands. "This close to Viyon," he said. But the hall was empty now, the small groups that formed earlier had dispersed during the course of Jared's unwarranted lecture.

"Come on man, what do you think? I survived that ride with you... I daresay I deserve some accolades," he reported to Viyon.

"Sure man! You do, thanks for the ride too."

"Aleck! Rowland! get in here now."

"Aaaaaarrrrrrggggh man! What does Bucky want this time around," Viyon groaned.

"I can hear you, you know? Get your skinny asses here now."

Jared and Viyon proceeded forward to the class with the enthusiasm of a slug. Coach Bucky was their class teacher and the Physical education teacher and the basketball team coach and he probably also heads the Parents-teachers association, but none of the students cared enough to find that out. The coach can be a sweet, sweet darling every once in a while, but the rest of the time, he is a total and complete pain in the ass.

"How nice of you two musketeers to show up in school. I thought you'd never come since you're five minutes late!" he turned to the class and back to them again like he had just remembered something: "Oh! And thanks for sparing the school garage, or what's left of it should I say. Now please move to your seats."

His expression turned pleasant once again as he continued; "We have a new student here with us today. They moved into town recently and she will be completing the rest of her academic year here with us. I believe I do not have to remind you to be nice and act like civilized humans".

He swept through the class with his eyes, settling on the students that have built a reputation for being bullies. "Now I'd like her to step forward and introduce herself properly to the rest of the class"

A beautiful brunette lady with the loveliest sets of green eyes that Viyon had ever seen stepped out to the front of the class. Viyon did not know he was staring until Bucky called him out.

"Mr. Aleck does need to exit the room or will a cold shower be okay?"

The class erupted in one huge volcano of laughter with Trevor spicing the situation with rowdy comments. Viyon's eye caught that of the new girl in front and she smiled at him; a kind, compassionate smile.

"Alright that's enough!" Bucky thundered from his table in front of the class. "One more word from your young man..." he pointed at a guy with spiky hair at the back of the class, one of Trevor's goons;

"... and you'd be serving detention after school with me. Now, wouldn't that be fun?"

The whole class fell silent almost immediately. Detention with Bucky was not something anyone looked forward to or walked into willingly. Where you'd serve your time doing lucrative activities with other teachers; Bucky made you sit in his office arranging a live album of pictures from when he was young, and he made it a point to narrate the stories behind each photograph. So, no matter how many times you might have heard the story before, Bucky made it a pleasure to always tell the story again with renewed zeal and glee.

When the class had quieted down, Bucky signaled the new girl to carry on with her introduction.

"Hi everyone, I'm Amanda Freeman. I moved down here last week from New Orleans with my parents because my dad got transferred from his job. But I'll have to say that from my short stay here, this town is beautiful and I look forward to getting to know more about the place and its people. Including you all, Thank you!"

Someone blew an air whistle when she was done, while someone else took advantage of the ruckus and screamed; "I look forward to knowing you too" and the class laughed. Nobody saw who said that, but the voice was all too familiar for anyone to miss it.

Amanda moved back to the class and took the seat directly beside Viyon. She smiled at him and tried to start a conversation but he couldn't get more than two words out of his mouth. Jared observed the situation from where he sat and passed Viyon a note that says:

I wish I was close to you so I can slap some sense into you, if you mess this up man, I'd put you on the next plane going to Antarctica.

Amanda got a peek at the note and smiled: "Sounds cold, don't you think?"

Viyon swallowed and stared at her before staring away quickly.

"I'm Amanda, which I'm sure you know. And you are?"

"Viyon," he whispered and looked away, concentrating on the book in front of him like it held the secret to finding out how to talk to girls.

"O.M.G!" she gasped. "You're Viyon, the Viyon Aleck? Wow!" her face lit up as she said it.

If she expected him to say anything in reply, Viyon certainly did not get the memo as he just smiled an awkward half-smile and just kept staring straight ahead.

"I've heard some things about you, good things actually and I'm happy to finally meet you. Heck! I'm in the same class as you. I'd hug you right now but I'm sure Bucky would not approve"

"Thank you," Viyon replied.

"Don't mind me, I get so excited at times. You don't seem to talk too much, do you? So, I'm guessing you're an introvert or you're shy. Which is it?"

"Shy."

"Aswan that's so cute. I'm sorry I shouldn't have done that; I'll stop talking now. It's just that I'm nervous, and I get really talkative when I'm like this. Do you want me to stop?"

"No, it's fine."

"My dad's a basketball fan. That's how I got to love the sport. If I had been a guy, or I was a foot or two taller, my dad would certainly have had me training to get signed up with a team by next summer. I'm sure you'd make it; you wouldn't have any problem getting a team to sign you up."

Viyon turned in his seat and looked at her then, looked her straight in the eye and gave her the biggest, widest smile he could have managed and said: "Thank you!"

"You're welcome!" she said. Then reached her hand across the table to get his hands in between hers and squeezed it gently.

Bucky turned from the board then, causing her to let go of his end and put an end to their conversation. He stared in their direction for a while, like he suspected what they had been up to while his back was turned to the class.

Jared had seen her holding Viyon's hands and stared at Viyon's face as if he was trying to send a telepathic message to him, Viyon finally looked in his direction and the expression on Jared's face made him know that he had seen the encounter and Viyon had a lot of telling to do when they meet in the cafeteria at break later in the day.

The rest of the class periods passed uneventfully the rest of the day and soon it was time to go on break. Viyon stayed back in class with the pretense of trying to finish up a note so that Jared would go on without him and he would be spared the embarrassment and tedious task of having to narrate his conversation with Amanda that morning to his friend. Jared however, would not let him off easily and appeared at his side.

"You're not walking out of this easy, young man. I know you're just pretending to write. Come on, up on your feet and out through the door, we've got some catching up to do," he said and smirked, clearly he was enjoying Viyon's discomfort.

"Don't you have something useful to do?"

"Nope! My whole life is dedicated to disturbing you."

Amanda walked into the class to pick up something from her seat and Jared seized the opportunity to get Viyon to move his butt out of the class. He raised his voice and started talking for Amanda's benefit. Viyon knew what he was going to do and intercepted him quickly.

"Come on man, let's go get lunch."

He stood up willingly knowing that if he does not, Jared would find a way to get Amanda involved and the last thing he wanted was to embarrass himself further with the pretty new girl in class. He barely heard a thing in class today, the entire time he was playing out different scenarios of how the conversation with Amanda could have gone and he beat himself up about being such a tongue-tied fool for not responding.

Damn! I even admitted to being shy. What's wrong with me?

"Earth to Viyon, let's go... the table at the cafeteria awaits our humble presence and the tales of our valiant victories. Now, do not keep us, me, and the table, waiting."

The cafeteria was packed full when they got there but their usual table was empty. Mrs. Perez was at the food counter when they got there, she lit up when she saw Viyon.

"Well hello young man, how are you?"

"I'm fine ma'am, how are you doing today Mrs. Perez?"

"I'm fine amigo, as you can see. You however look like you need some meat on those bones."

Viyon smiled. Mrs. Perez never believes he has enough meat on his bones. She's always asking him to eat so that he would be strong and manly.

"The usual huh?" she filled a plate for him and added an extra bun. "There you go..."

"Thanks!"

She smiled her most heartwarming motherly smile at him as he took the tray from her, Jared's mom had packed him sandwiches and some homemade juice so he did not need to get anything from the cafeteria. They were halfway through the hall to their usual table when a familiar voice called out Viyon's name and made his heart skip a dozen beats.

"Act natural don't mess this up for us man," Jared whispered.

"How the hell I am I supposed to act when I do not even remember how to breathe?" he replied.

Amanda approached their table with her lunch tray in her hands: "Can I join you? That is if you do not mind, I couldn't find anywhere else."

Viyon looked around the cafeteria and was about to point out a couple of places where she could have sat when Jared stepped on his toe and replied to her. "We do not mind; we would love to have you sit with us."

"Thanks…" she tilted her head to the side like she was trying to remember the name when Jared filled it in for her.

"Jared…" he said.

"Thank you, Jared, Viyon?"

"Sorry, I was lost in thoughts there for a minute" She nodded her head towards the seat as a way of reminding him about her question.

"Oh! I'm sorry, yeah you can join us."

Jared was the perfect gentleman guiding her to her seat with her lunch. Conversations moved around the table with Viyon inputting when he absolutely needed to. Amanda asked a question about a subject and Jared suggested that she ask him, she reached her hands out to tap him and he dropped his fork.

"Oh my, I'm sorry about that."

"No, I was clumsy I'll just get another one," he left the table and returned a few minutes later with another fork.

"Jared tells me you're a guru at Chemistry, is that so?"

"I can't vouch for anything Jared says to you…"

"So, are you good at chemistry or not?"

"I will try."

"Oh please, don't listen to him. He's just awfully modest. Man's a beast at it," Jared said, which caused Amanda to laugh.

The rest of the lunch break went smoothly except for the few more times when Viyon's fork fell from his hand and he had to go get a replacement from the kitchen.

"I think she likes you man," Jared said, when they were alone.

"I'm sure she thinks I'm a freak, an idiot, and a sore loser."

"Her words or yours?"

"She doesn't have to say it, I can feel it, I know. I dropped my fork a thousand times, spilled a drink on my shirt and I could not even hold eye contact with her when I'm talking. She definitely thinks I'm a complete moron."

"Wow, I never thought the day would come when I would be able to tell you this; but it is with great pleasure that I announce to you that you are dumb."

Viyon did not say anything in response so he continued.

"Open your eyes man, the signs are every day."

"I don't know what you're talking about. I'd be surprised if she ever talks to me again."

"Yeah me too, let's go home man. Let's call it a day."

Chapter Five

Coach Bucky walked into the gym looking prepped up and ready to hit the tracks like he always looks every day after school at B-ball practice. He was dressed in a yellow tracksuit with white and black highlights in his arms. On his head, he had a camouflage bandana tied around the circumference of his hand. His official whistle is hung on his neck and it never leaves that spot, not even after practice. He was wearing his special sneakers today which meant that they were going to have a long session today.

The players in the gym were clustered in groups having their usual chit chat, everyone on one wing of the hall with a friend talking about whatever tickles their fancy. The students used this time to relax and warm up before the coach come and they were doing just that before the shrill sound of Bucky's whistle penetrated the air, shattering the serenity of the atmosphere. At once, each person stopped whatever activity they were engaged in beforehand, each looking towards the door to find out the source of the disturbance.

"Gather round suckers, I've got big news!"

Coach Bucky announced at the entrance to the gym. As was his tradition, he called the team any name he deemed fit, when he felt like; Suckers, Dimwits, Dickheads, and a variety of others. On a rougher, more terrible day, the team gets a name that alerts them to the situation at hand; that is, his mood. On a slightly less bad day, the team gets a slightly less awful name. No one knows what name the team receives on Bucky's good day. As far as they know, Bucky never has a good day.

"Centerfield everyone. Hey, Stilinski, get your slimy ass off those benches now!"

The students filed out from their previous positions in the hall to the center where Bucky was standing and stood out in a straight line in front of him. Previous experiences have taught them never to form a circle or crescent around them. They had no sooner finished conveying than Bucky assigned another workout to them.

"Take fifty laps, everybody, let's go."

"Freeman, raise those legs like you've got oxygen in you and not gas implant."

"Aleck, come on! What did you have for breakfast, breastmilk? Because you're running like you're going to pass out in the hall right now. Give it your all man, even if it means you drop down while you're at it, at least you'd know you did your best."

"Yeah, Stilinski, that's good. Come on, I like it. Go... go... go!"

"Rowland? What the hell do you think you're doing? Get your ass up man!"

"Alright, that's enough!" he blew into the whistle to signal the end of that round.

"50 pushups everybody, let's go!" Bucky blew into the whistle again and as one all the students went down on their hands, with their bodies stretched out behind them. Bucky did the counting while they did the push-ups.

"Mr. Roman, do you plan on leaving that spot anytime soon, or would you like some time alone?"

"Come on! Keep going... 32...! 33...! 34...!"

"Stilinski, stop being a disappointment will ya?"

"You want the girls clamoring for you but you don't want to put in the work? Get to work lazy ass!"

"Alright that's it!" he blows the whistle. "Take a rest lady, we start practice in five."

The guys waited for the coach to get out the door before dropping into a pile on the floor. As was the norm with them; whenever they are on a break before practice after the warm-ups, the coach excuses them to do whatever they please with their time while he sorts himself out.

"Damn man, I can barely feel my hands," Roman said.

"Makes me wonder if he was a donkey in his past life."

"The man's worse than a donkey if you ask me."

"… But you got to admit that he does his job well."

"Phuuuuuuuuuuuuuuuuuuuuuuuu," the shrill sound from Bucky's whistle pierced the air, calling the attention of the players to order.

"Two teams: Aleck, Stilinski your power forwards," he pointed at a redhead to his left. "Your point guard. Rowland, you assist him. Everyone else, to your normal position."

"Pass the rock to Freeman… Aleck takes it to the hole…!"

"Nice basket!"

The game lasted for about thirty minutes after which the coach made them play twenty-one, all the players on the court defending the net, while a player tries to score a basket. Each player got a turn before Bucky called an end to it. After practice, he assessed who did well and who needed to improve on what. The difference between how he delivered both compliment and rebuke was very slim, but they understood his point anyway and grabbed unto what little they could hold on to.

"Have a seat. There's going to be a junior championship Basketball game at the end of the term," the players cheered.

"Yeah! It's the same one you know of and you have been waiting for. I do not need to remind you that representatives from most of the top schools and colleges will be present; they'd not just be here for entertainment; they will be scouting for the finest talent to add to their team. Now, I'd say this just once, don't ever ask me to repeat it but all of you here are the finest there is in town," the players cheered again and Bucky gave them some time to quiet down before he continued.

"As I was saying before I was rudely interrupted, it is only natural that I would expect you to bring that cup home and that every one of you gets signed with a team or receives a measly scholarship at the very least; that's the least you could do. So, sissies, you have your work cut out for you."

He picked up his folder, ticked the attendance for the people that were present at the practice for the day, then bid them goodbye.

"Adios civilians! See you bright and early tomorrow. I do not want any crappy story of cramps or the likes, and do not even think of missing practices for anything this week, the dates with your girlfriends will have to wait. That's enough pep talk for one evening, sleep tight, don't let the bugs bite," he grinned at them then took his leave.

The gym became a hive of boys changing out of their sportswear into their regular clothes and discussing their plans for the rest of the day. A couple of the guys said their goodbyes and left, leaving a handful of the players at the gym.

"I'll see you later man, I got the week's shift at the restaurant so I got to go, but we'll catch up later. I'll come by the house."

"Okay sure, I won't wait up."

"Like hell, you will, you better believe that I'll show up because I will. I need help with my chemistry and the assignment is due like I didn't know yesterday? Get some milk and cookies ready because it's gonna be a long night and please, no Star Wars. Hold on! You know what? Star Wars can stay, all work and no play yeah?"

"I don't even know why I put up with you."

"Probably because I make your existence less boring?"

Viyon laughed and tried to punch him but Jared had already anticipated it and dodged easily. Jared waited as Viyon gathered his things together in his bag, lifted it onto his shoulders then exited the gym together.

"I was thinking…"

"Oh no, this can't be good," Jared said.

"Hahaha…!!! It's nothing, just that I haven't heard you say anything about Cindy in the past week. Trouble in paradise?"

"I knew you were going to ask."

"So, spill it."

"I don't know, I'm just not feeling it…"

"Hun hun…!" Viyon raised a brow at him in a what-have-you-done-again-this-time kinda way.

"Don't give me that look, I didn't do anything," Viyon's brows went even higher and Jared sighed, closing his eyes and hunching his shoulders like the weight of the world rested on him, then he finally said; "I lied"

"I could tell. Alright, out with it. What happened?"

"Technically we did not break up because we were never dating, but she… she's going to prom with Michael."

"Prom?"

"Dude, have you been living under a rock?"

"Nope, I just do not pay attention to the notice board or any of those things that those girls with pompoms do."

"Well news flash Viyon, prom is at the end of the month."

"Now that's interesting! And he asked a month ahead? Wow! Guy's a sharpshooter."

"Dude, not helping."

"Oh yeah, sorry. Who's he anyway?"

"Yeah right? I mean, who is he think he is?"

"No seriously, who's Michael? Does the school here?"

"I think so… He's only the football captain for the school's football team…"

"Oh! That guy?" Viyon looked like he was trying to find the right words to use. "You're better than him… mentally!"

Jared's countenance seems to have lightened up slightly so he continued; "I mean, dude cannot even hold a gaze for more than a couple of seconds. You're way tougher than that."

"I know you're trying to make me feel better, but damn it's working! Keep it coming."

"That's it, man, I'm all out. That's all I can manage."

Jared dug his elbow into Viyon's stomach, making him bend over and groan. "I'll take that one because you're currently going through a phase."

"Like hell I am, but I met someone else though and I'm going in for the kill."

"Again? Let's not, let's not do that again this time. You went in for the kill the previous time and she ran off. How about you take it nice and slow."

"Like with you and Amanda?"

"What has that got to this with this?"

"Everything man, we cannot both suck at getting a girl, especially one that is so into you like Amanda is."

They got to the front of the restaurant where they both work, making them pause the conversation.

"I got to go man, but that does not mean you escaped this talk. We will continue this discussion when I come over in the evening. Say hi to Mrs. Aleck, let her know I'll be over for dinner tonight."

"Sure, I'll see you. We'll be fine as long as her husband doesn't do anything stupid."

"Her husband huh? Is that bad?"

"Yeah, I don't think I have a dad."

Jared clapped him on the back in a brotherly manner and said; "You'll be fine bro. I'm here. Not here, as in the building or physical location. Whatever man, you get what I mean."

"Yeah, I do, see you later tonight."

"I'll be there," they shook hands and went their separate ways.

Viyon woke up to a loud knock at the door. He sat up groggily, pulled on his slippers before paddling downstairs to get the door. The house was empty when he got back; his mom had left him a note on the dining table and a bowl of lasagna alongside it, which he microwaved and ate for lunch.

He wondered who it was at the door by this time of the day and at first, his drowsy mind went to mom, he had totally forgotten that mom had informed him that she would be on call tonight and so would not be coming back home for the night.

"Who's it?"

"It's Jared!"

"Oh! Come on in," Viyon said and opened the door.

"What took you so long? Have you got someone else here?"

"No, just me."

"Your mom's working the night shift tonight?"

"You said it."

"Aww man, I didn't get dinner. Maybe we'll just order pizza?"

Viyon stood up and went into the kitchen to microwave what's left of the lasagna, replying to Jared as he did. "No need for that, mom left me a bowl of lasagna. There were some left, we could eat that."

"Cool! So, I ran into Freeman at the restaurant today. He was there with a fine babe. She looks like a high school student to me, but I don't think she goes to our school. Man's a badass, still has the time to catch up on the fun even with our crazy-ass schedule."

Viyon made a grunting sound from the kitchen as a way of letting Jared know that he could hear him and he was with him in the conversation.

"Anyways that's not the reason I started this talk," Jared continued. "We got talking and he mentioned that exams would be starting two weeks before the prom, which is just a week from now and also around the same time for the junior championship match."

"WHAT?!" Viyon choked out.

"That was my exact reaction. I felt like I had just been punched in the guts by Mohammed Ali. These things should not really be a surprise to us if we paid attention to details but we do not and so it's alarming."

"I think I'm gonna have a panic attack."

"Seriously, then you better call 911 because I'll probably end up in an emergency room. How can you even say that? You can ace this man; you need to stop thinking less of yourself and start recognizing how much potential you have bottled up inside of you."

"I don't know what you're talking about."

"You are natural at sports; you excel in your studies. Fine, the last test, what did you do? Superb! That's how you did it. Now stop being fidgety and get your shit together," he paused for dramatic effect then threw his hands up and screamed; "Who… hood! I'm on fire tonight. I really should consider being a motivational speaker."

"I feel I just get lucky; I do not know why you see me as a prodigy of some sort."

"Like hell, you're a prodigy and if you keep trying to act meek and humble, you're gonna piss me off. Let's just do chemistry, shall we?"

The timer on the microwave went off, alerting them to the bowl of lasagna sitting pretty inside it, getting warmed up.

"… That is after we've had dinner, of course."

"You think that's a good idea?"

"Hey! Hey! Don't go all shrink-is on me right now. I'm starving and I'm gonna eat that meal or else, whatever chemical jargons you're gonna be spilling out of your enlightened, educated mouth for the next hour is just gonna pass over my head and go out right through that window," he said, pointing at the window by the dining where he had placed his textbooks.

"… And if that happens, you can bet that I'm gonna show up here again tomorrow night or any other night after that until I learn what I need to; So, lasagna or not?"

Viyon doubled up with laughter, "Help yourself, you know the way. The plates are in the top cabinet to the right. Mom did a sort of mini rearrangement two days ago. Cutleries are in the drawer beneath the microwave, the trays are easy to spot, you shouldn't miss them."

"I'm hungry, I don't need this info."

Viyon raised his hands as if in surrender, "Go right ahead then, we'll start in ten minutes. That's enough time for you to get your food down right?"

"Yeah, thanks coach!" Jared replied sarcastically, which made Viyon laugh again as he passed him to the kitchen.

"How do I work this thing man? It won't budge."

"What's that?"

"The refrigerator."

"Just press and pull," he paused for a minute before asking: "You good, have you opened it?"

"Yeah sure, thanks," Jared replied.

Jared walked into the sitting room a few minutes later with a plate of lasagna in one hand and a bottle of water in the other.

"My mom would throw a fit if she caught me behaving so 'unbecoming'," he inflected his voice to sound like his mom: "Jared Theodore Rowland! Get your meal to the dining table this instant."

"Wow!" Viyon exclaimed. "Do you always have your meals at the dining."

"Only when she's around; which is most of the time. Sometimes I envy you, your mom's barely around and you get this really cool apartment all to yourself."

"Yeah… my life's great!" Viyon said in a dry tone.

Jared made a face like he was going to ask Viyon what that comment was about, then decided against it.

"Can we watch Star Wars?"

"I thought you wanted to study chemistry."

"We're teenagers man, we're too young to be saddened by the realities of the world, we'll do that when we're forty, so for now, can I just enjoy my plate of lasagna with sci-fi make-believe of the realities of another imaginative world huh? Is that too much to ask?"

"I don't know what has gotten into you, but I'm just going to pass it off as you've had a difficult day."

"I certainly have, but I want to talk about it after I've had a meal and I'm watching Star Wars," he said and gave Viyon a wide grin.

"Suit yourself, man. The remote is right in front of you."

"Now that's a good host. Your old man's not around?"

"I don't care where he is," Viyon said.

"Yup, I got it. I won't ask again."

Jared finished his meal shortly after but at that time both boys were already too engrossed in Star Wars to even remember why they were there in the first place.

"Ouch! That has got to hurt," Jared exclaimed.

"Darth Vader is a beast, I can't wait to see him meet his waterloo," this time it was Viyon speaking.

"Would you look at that? It's past ten, on a school night! My mom would most certainly burst through that door anytime soon, that is after she harasses my phone with a thousand calls starting now…"

As if on cue, Jared's phone rings and he moves into the kitchen to answer the call. From his place on the sofa in the sitting room, Viyon could hear him trying to pacify his mom. It seemed that approach did not work as he pulled the Viyon's-home-alone card and as always Mrs. Rowland asked to speak with Viyon.

"Viyoooooooooooooooon…!" Jared called, dragging out the name "Mom wants to speak with you."

Jared gives him a look that very much says 'back up my story' before handing the phone over to him.

"You owe me a big time," Viyon mouthed as he took the phone. "I know," Jared replied.

"Hi Mrs. Rowland!"

Brief pause.

"Yes ma'am, my mum is working the night shift at the hospital tonight."

Brief pause.

"No ma'am, there's no babysitter here. My dad should have been back by now."

A long pause this time, which has Jared making facial gestures at Viyon, to which he replied with an equally dramatic facial gesture in return.

"That's very kind of your ma'am, we'll be over in ten minutes," Viyon said and ended the call.

"Thanks, man, I just dodged a bullet with that one. I kinda knew she was going to ask you to go sleepover at our house, sorry I dragged you into this."

"It's no bother, this should be fun! I'll grab what I need for school tomorrow and we should be out of here in no time."

"Okay…! I'll be right here. Do you want to drive?"

"You bet I want to," he climbed up to his room and returned a few minutes later with a backpack slang on one shoulder. "I'm ready."

Viyon did not bother leaving a note for his father to inform him of his impromptu sleepover arrangement over at the Rowland's, he guessed there would be no need for that as his father would probably not show up at the house that night; turns out, he was right. Justin was a hundred miles from home, snuggled nicely under sheets with a lady who would soon be the cause of a major turnaround for the Alecks.

Chapter Six

"Honey, wake up! You passed out on the couch. You looked so exhausted, what do they have you people doing down in that school," Viyon's mom said, as she woke him up and tried to help him gather his things together.

"Aaaargh! Your room is a mess. Have you cleaned up all this week? And you need to take a shower young man. You'd rest better when you, now up you go."

"Aaaaaarrrrgggghhhh!" Viyon grunts as he rises up from the couch. "Is it a school day today?"

"No, it is not. It's Saturday."

"Thank Goodness," he said and plopped right back into the couch.

"Viyon Timothy Aleck, would you be so kind as to get off my couch and take a shower? Trust me, you need it."

"Mom…!!!"

"… And what have you been up to, you smell like a horse, the whole place is a mess and Jared's not down here yet, which means he is equally having an episode over at his house."

"We're having one hell of a week that's what. There's a junior championship match coming up at the end of the month and the coach has got us practicing every day after school, back to back. Not to mention that our final exams and the school prom are also about the same period. Oh yeah, and I worked the shift at work this past weekend so I'm as tired as four donkeys and a horse put together. Please, mom, don't make me stand, or turn or take a shower or generally do anything that involves not dreaming."

"I'm making pancakes..."

"Can I eat them while I'm sleeping?"

"... with cherry toppings and cheese as a side."

"I'm not buying..."

"I'll make that fruit compote that you like with some grilled chicken wings..."

"How can I argue with chicken wings? You strike a hard bargain, ma'am. I now evacuate your couch."

"You're so cute," she pecks him on the top of his head, his cheeks, and his nose before releasing him to go.

"Mom, I'm grown now. You can't call me cute or kiss my entire face like that. I could have a girlfriend."

"Hmmm, really?"

"Why do I sense sarcasm in that tone? You don't think I can have a girlfriend? You don't think I can talk to a girl?

"Not smelling like that you don't. Besides, I do not think you've spoken to anyone of the opposite sex since Shelley," his mom said and winked on her way to the kitchen.

"Ahhhhhhhh! You knew, and you acted oblivious all this while."

"Of course, I knew, it's pretty hard to hide that you had a crush on your babysitter when you glow up every time she shows up. I bet you two even kissed."

"Whaaaaaaaaat…?! That's gross," Viyon said in an inflected tone.

"The Hun…! Yeah, you would know that wouldn't you?"

"What do you mean?"

"I mean, you certainly kissed her, or she kissed you. I don't know which happened, but I'm sure one did. You just gave it away with your 'Whaaaaaaaaaaaaaat?'"

"Why am I even talking about this stuff with you, it's straight out awkward."

"You brought it up?"

"That's it, I'm going to shower. I'm done discussing my relationships with you," he said as he climbed up the stairs to his room.

"… or lack of it," his mom whispered, loud enough for him to hear.

"I can't hear you…" he shouted back and turned on the shower.

* * *

"Hello Jared!"

"Holy freckles, you scared the pants off me. Not literary though," he tried to regain composure and continued.

"What are you doing here?"

"I came to get food? pretty obvious if you ask me."

"Oh yeah, certainly. I knew that I just... arm... I was just checking to make sure you remembered why you're here," he slapped himself on his laps. "That sounds stupid, even to me."

"It sure does," they held each other's gaze for a second, then burst out in laughter.

"Truth is, if I was being completely honest, I wouldn't just come here to eat. I heard the food's great here and all but I learned that you both work here and I was hoping to see him here."

Jared looked around like he was trying to figure out who it was that she was talking about, after looking pointlessly through the restaurant, the look on Amanda's face told him he knew who she was talking about and he just acted dumb again.

"I did it again didn't I?" she simply nodded her head and laughed in response. "So, where is he?" she asked?

"Viyon? Probably at home, or at the park or practicing Basketball somewhere. But I'd stake my money at home. At least I'm almost sure he's not out on a date or anything," he looked at her face and said,

"Oh, sorry. He's definitely not out on a date. I know that."

"It's okay. I know that too."

"You do?"

"Well, it's not like I know for sure, I'm just concurring with what you said."

"Can I get you a cup of coffee or tea, water, anything?"

"Yes please, coffee is fine."

"Okay... I'll be right back," he said and dashed off behind the sales counter.

The moment Jared was behind the counter and safely out of Amanda's sight, he took out his phone and put a call across to Viyon. He usually would have sent a text, but the issue at hand was a pressing one, or so he wanted Viyon to believe. The phone rang for a while before Viyon got to it. His voice sounded groggy and lazy, like he was just waking up. Jared felt bad for what he was about to do but his guilt lasted only a nanosecond and he was back on plan.

"Hi Viyon!"

"Hey... what's going on man?"

"You sound sleepy, what were you up to?"

"I just got out of the shower, my mom made me do it though"

"Perfect...!"

"What do you mean "perfect"?"

"I hate to bother you but you're needed at the restaurant ASAP. Don't ask; Just dress up and hit the road. I think you have about five minutes. Oh, and Viyon, you might want to look good. See ya."

"Hold on… Jared?" He dropped the receiver. "Shit!"

Viyon was dressed and ready to go in a couple of minutes, "Mom…!" he yelled at the door.

"I'll have breakfast when I'm back, Jared called, he says I'm needed at the restaurant. I'll stop by and find out what's going on, then pop right back."

"Be safe honey," his mom yelled back from the kitchen.

Viyon was halfway across the porch when a thought flashed through his mind and he ran back into the house. "Mom…?"

"I'm over here…"

"Can I borrow your car please?"

"You know how to drive?"

"It's only a matter of time before I learn if Jared knows how to, don't you think? He taught me."

If his mom was thinking something, her face certainly did not show it as she stared blankly at him, a million thoughts running through her mind as she did. "That's fine honey, you can take the car. But you get a single scratch on it and you can kiss your college funds goodbye. You'll be down at the barber's shop down at fifth avenue before you know it."

"Thanks, mom, I'll keep that in mind," he said as he pecked her cheeks before dashing out the front door again. He came back a few seconds later to grab her keys off the table, "I forgot these," he held the key up to her. "Bye now, see you later."

Viyon felt the situation was not as serious as Jared painted it, but he hurried all the same. There was no telling this guy and he would rather be safe than sorry. He was at the restaurant exactly five minutes later. Quickly, he turned off the ignition, came out of the car, and made straight for the door. Once inside the dashed behind the counter to Jared's station, but found it empty.

"Hey Jones, have you seen Jared?"

"He's over there on table 22, is there a problem?"

"I'm about to find out. Thanks!"

Jones said something in reply but Viyon had started out in the direction he pointed out and totally missed what was being said. Viyon got to the table and almost passed out from shock had Jared not stood up to help him.

"Hi Viyon," Amanda said, smiling at him.

Jared stood to one side, looking smug like a proud coach would if his team was whooping asses on the field. Viyon finally regained his tongue and spoke; "Hi… I didn't think I'd find you here. You look nice. Can you excuse me for a minute, please? Jared, Jones needs you at the counter, noontime rush I guess…"

Jared looked around at the quiet restaurant, there was definitely no noontime rush, plus it was already past noon. He was going to make a smart-ass comment in that regard, but one looked at Viyon's face and he decided against it.

"Errrr.... Yeah, that's true. Tell him I'll be right there"

"I think he needs you now," Viyon said, nodding his head in the direction of the counter.

"Sure, Amanda if you'll please excuse me."

Both guys scrambled out of sight, once out of sight, Viyon backed Jared into a corner.

"You mind telling me what's going on?"

"I had to get you down here ASAP and the only way to ensure that was to make you believe it was urgent."

"Wow, that makes sense…"

"I know, it was reckless and stupid, and I'm sorry. But she showed up here looking for you man, and as a gentleman, it was against my honor to let her leave like that when you're so close. This is your chance man, Prom night's calling."

"You owe me big time; I don't even know why I put up with you."

"You owe me man; you would not be thinking about me when you get all kissy mushy with her."

Viyon shot him a wicked look which made him retreat and throw both hands up as if in surrender, "Okay, okay! I'll back up."

"Thanks, bills on you by the way. I was so much in a rush; I didn't think, I would come out with a wallet"

"What the…"

"Thanks, I owe you one," Viyon said, whilst patting him on the back.

Jones stuck his head through the opening connecting the counter to the kitchen to check on both of them His face took on a puzzling look when he saw Viyon's arm around Jared's neck. "What's going on?" he asked.

"It's nothing bro, we're good."

"Good, cause the lady at the table looks like she's about to fly," he stuck his head through the opening again and said; "by the fly, I mean leave. She's about to leave."

"We get it, Jones, thank you."

Viyon walked back into the restaurant, trying to summon up all the courage and composure that he was so far from feeling. He got to the table as Amanda was trying to get up.

"Not about to make a run for it, are we?" he said.

"I was definitely going to do that," she replied.

"I'm sorry about the whole drama, Jared made me believe it was a dire situation to get me down here."

"Would you have come otherwise?"

"Probably not, I get tongued tied and frightened to death whenever I'm around you. I was sure you'd never speak to me again after the last encounter we had."

"I do not remember any of what you're talking about."

"Well, I basically dropped my fork a million times and had to get it changed, and I spilled drinks on myself. That's the entire story."

She threw her head back and laughed long and hard. "I remember now, but it's not exactly as you paint it to be."

Jared came by with two tall glasses of juice and a menu, "Can I get you two anything?" he asked.

"I'll take the steak, medium rare and barbecue sauce as a side dip," Viyon said and winked at him.

"I'll take the same," Amanda said.

"Alright, I'll be right back. I hope you have an enjoyable stay," he stressed the word 'enjoyable' while staring at Viyon before he left to attend to their order.

He returned shortly with their order, "There you go," he said, placing the plates on the table, in front of both people, then took a bow and left.

"You do not seem so shy anymore, what changed?" Amanda asked, picking up on the conversation they were having before their meal came.

"Honestly, I do not know."

She smiled and reached her hands across the table to grab both of his hands in hers. They continued their talk over the meal, discussing everything from childhood experiences to junior high school, to plans for the future and more. It took three missed calls from Viyon's mom to alert him of how much time they've spent hanging out.

"Would you look at that? It's past four. My mom's gonna be over her mind with worry. I've had the most enjoyable time; it was fun doing this with you. Thanks."

"So… you want to do this again sometime?"

"Yeah, definitely! Shoot…!" He slaps himself on the forehead with his palm, "I'm such an idiot. That should have been my line, I'm sorry. But I'd really love to go out with you again, that is if you want to…"

"Are you kidding? Of course, I want to. Just call me and let me know when."

"I… will, after I get your number," he held out his phone for her to type in her digits which caused her to smile and blush.

Viyon walked her to the door and hugged her goodbye, all the time aware of Jared's piercing gaze following them all the way out. He did not need a soothsayer to know that Jared would be on his tail all the way home. He would want to hear every detail of their outing tonight, maybe not every, but the major, juicy, part of it.

Viyon turned back to the direction of the restaurant, through the clear glass structure covering the place, he could see Jared. Both people made eye contact and Viyon nodded at Jared to let him know he was leaving. Jared made a 'call me' sign, then nodded right back.

"I better have a good story to tell mom when I get back or I'm screwed," he muttered to himself as he got in the car and drove off.

* * *

The house was quiet when Viyon got back, not like his mom would usually leave the home theater on and jam to music or anything, but the place felt eerie and weird. He could feel that something just wasn't right, the whole place was strangely calm.

"Mom?" he called out; slowly and quietly at first, then louder.

He got into the house and headed straight for the kitchen, but his mom was not there. "What was I thinking, of course, she'd have left the kitchen a long time."

He checked the sitting room; her room upstairs, his room, and every other place in the house he could think of to check, but did not find her. That's when he got really worried.

"Moooooooooooom!!!" he shouted. He could not remember her telling him that she would be going out today. And this most certainly was not the first time he'd come back and she wouldn't be at home, but this time felt different. Something was amiss and not knowing what it was, was killing him.

"I'm here honey, in the backyard."

He tore through the house to the backyard and found her sitting on the lawn, her bare feet on the grass. Her eyes were red and wet and slightly puffy, which meant that she had been crying. It made sense now why she would refuse to answer all the while he had been screaming at her name. She was probably trying to put herself together and act tough and strong for his sake.

"Mom?"

"Honey…" she said with forced enthusiasm. "You're back."

"Yeah, I am. Please don't do that."

"Don't do what?" she asked sincerely.

"I know something's up, you were crying…" he saw the look on her face and interrupted her before she even had the chance to say anything. "… Don't try to deny it. What are you going to say now, that the dust got in your eye? Or are you're having an allergic reaction? Come on mom, I'm not a kid anymore. You've been crying and I know that because your eyes are red and puffy and your lashes are still wet."

Having been stripped of whatever lie she could have used as a defense, Miriam decided there was no need to try and put up an act anymore. "I'm sorry dear, I do not want you to worry your pretty head over all these. You're a smart kid and I'm grateful as can be that I have you."

"Now you're scaring me."

She drew him close and hugged him tightly. "We're getting divorced. Your dad and I," she whispered quietly, so quietly he would have missed it if he wasn't paying attention.

His reaction came slowly, dully; as if in some way, he knew this; had expected that it would happen and it was only just playing out. Viyon waited to feel something, anything at all: rage, betrayal, sadness, confusion, anything. But he came up blank. He stared blankly into space behind their backyard, still holding on tightly to his mom.

For Miriam however, it was a different case altogether, the flood gates open and she started tearing up again. Against himself, Viyon was outraged. He was mad at his dad for causing her this much pain. He was mad at his mom for letting dad affect her this way. He felt if she should have any reaction at all to all these, it should be pure, undiluted, anger. And he was mad at himself for getting angry at his mom on account of his no-good dad. Dad has put them through a lot over the years, causing Viyon to conclude that he does not deserve her tears or anything from her at all.

"It's alright mom. We'll be fine."

"He was cheating; he came by earlier to move his things. That's when he gave me the cock and bull story of needing to go our separate ways," she sniffed, and Viyon held out his handkerchief to her, "Thanks, honey. He said we've grown distant and he's with someone else now. But what I can't seem to understand is why he would do this to us. Why now?"

At a loss for what to say, Viyon simply drew her closer and hugged her tighter. She needed to be pacified and made her feel better. She probably wanted to be assured of his decency, maybe tell her that he is a good man and he will realize he has made a mistake and come back but Viyon wasn't feeling like doing or saying any of those things to her. If anything at all, he was glad that his dad had finally gone from their lives.

"It's alright mom, everything's going to be just fine."

They sat outside there for a long time not saying anything to each other, each engrossed in their own thoughts and concern for the future. Viyon drank in the tranquility of nature around them, hoping that somehow it would calm the torrent of emotions raging inside him.

The sound of the telephone ringing inside the house was a rude intrusion to their moment. Somehow, it feels as if everything they've known before now, happened hundreds of light-years ago. Life took on a much bumpier turn in the ride for them; more so for Miriam, than for Viyon. For Viyon, he could be dancing in the streets right now as he has never felt the need for any close bonding or mutual activity of any sort with his father.

All his life, it has been his mom who made an effort to show up at his recitals, school plays, and basketball games despite her busy schedule. His dad was a hulking figure; always sulking and smashing everything in his path, so Viyon had learned early to keep his distance. So much so, that he doesn't notice his absence when he's not around, the same way he would not miss him now.

His major concern however was for his mom, who despite all of Justin's, his dad, cantankerous attitude still believed there was good in him and that he would someday reach within himself and reveal that part to the world. Sadly, however, the day never came and that revelation never happened. Viyon understands that his mom is trying to take in the harsh truth of the situation and feels sad for her.

"Come on mom, let's go inside. You'll catch a cold here."

"Thanks."

Not that he was expecting much from her, but the fact that her communication has been reduced to the use of a single word, revived the annoyance that Viyon felt towards his father.

"Go to bed mom, I'll take care of everything else. Let me know if you need something."

"I will, thanks, honey. I hate for you to see me like this."

"Don't say that. I love your mom, now close your eyes and try and get some sleep, you should feel better when you wake up," or so he hopes. He turned off the lights on his way out of the room and shut the door behind him as he left.

* * *

"Viyon, wait up."

Viyon turned back to see Jared running across the hall to him with his backpack in his hand, swinging from side to side as he ran. His hair got in his face as he ran and he stopped so he could push it back with one hand.

"Phew…! I… I… just give me a second," he turned his back to him then breathed slowly in and out a couple of times before turning back to him. "I've been trying to call you, tried your cellphone a couple of times then I called the house line and nobody answered. What's happening? Are you good?"

"My parents are getting divorced," Viyon said dryly, his face a blank stare, not betraying any of the emotions he was feeling.

"Aaaaaaaaaahhh!" Jared gasped and pulled him along into a corner. "How can you say that so casually? How are you holding up?"

"I'm fine," Viyon said, pulling free of Jared's grasp. "Does it not look like I am?"

Jared just stood there saying nothing, staring at Viyon with a soulful look in his eyes. He knew his friend was in deep shit and he was trying to reach out, but Viyon wasn't one for expressing how he really felt. At a loss for what to do to comfort him, he reached his hands out to clasp Viyon on the back, then pulled him into a tight hug. "You'll be fine bro, I'm here for you anytime," he whispered.

"Thanks! It's still low key so…"

"Totally… my lips are sealed."

The bell went off in the hall, alerting both persons that the classes were about to start, side by side they walked into the class to face another regular day like they used to; classes, practice after school, work, play, and party. Unaware that their whole life was about to be messed up and their entire routine, torn apart.

Chapter Seven

"Good morning Mrs. Aleck, please come with me…
right this way, He's waiting for you."

The secretary led her through the lobby through
a series of hallways, past a major workstation
organized into different work cubicles, took a left
turn after that then walked straight down a hallway
with offices at the sides until they got to a door
marked 'Conference room C'."

"Go on in ma'am, he's there. Would you like a
cup of coffee or anything?" the secretary asked.

Miriam thought about it. She was about to
decline at first; she was here on some really pressing
matters and did not want to indulge their little
conveniences such as coffee, but then again, she was
going into a legal war of some sort and needs to
employ all arsenals at her disposal, part of which
includes a sharp and active mind, hence the coffee.

"Yes please, I would love a cup, black. Thank
you!"

"It's my pleasure ma'am, I'll get it to you shortly"

Miriam watched the secretary go as she took a
minute to put herself together. This was a new face at
Roberts Specters and associates. Miriam had become

fast friends with the previous secretary during the course of her occasional visits to the firm, sometimes she'd stay with her at the reception and they'd chat about events that happened in their daily lives while she's waiting for Roberts to be done. She became a client of Roberts' after she got employed at the state's hospital in town, then they became friends when she got married to his former colleague and friend.

The story of how Robert's and Justin's relationship turned sour was one that Miriam could not talk about, being oblivious of the details herself. At first, Miriam had some misgivings about having Roberts represent her as her divorce attorney judging his history with Justin, that same history which became the major reason she decided to come to him in the end. If she was going to have a chance to win Justin at this and come out with as little casualty as possible to both her mental and physical wellbeing, she would not hesitate to take it and Roberts was her best bet.

Knowing Justin, he'd want to drag this out long and hard until she's tired and too stressed to fight back, then he'd rip her of everything she's got. She shook her head then adjusted the sleeves of her top, raising her head so that her chin was pointed and her jaw set tight, she pouted. She would never let him do that. She would not let him take the one thing that she valued more than anything in the world, Viyon. She was prepared to give him a fight to the end, and a fierce one at that. With that, she opened the door and entered.

Roberts was seated at the end of a long row of chairs arranged around a long rectangular table, the table and the chairs could hold at least six persons so Miriam guessed this should be a mini-conference room for meeting clients and signing agreements, rather than holding board meetings.

Roberts stood up when he saw her and walked across the room to her, he stretched out his hand for a handshake then thought better of it and pulled her into a hug, kissing her forehead in an affectionate way like a father would do.

"How are you, Miriam? You look good."

"What do you think? I can't wait for this to be all over, that's how I am. I'm holding up though if that's what you're asking," she replied.

"I can tell. Please, have a seat," he said, guiding her to the seat closest to the one he vacated a few minutes before.

"Thank you, I noticed Maryann wasn't at the front desk when I came in, did she quit?"

"Yes, painfully so, on my part that is; because we asked her to stay, even promised her a raise in her salary but her mind was made up and she needed to go."

"I see. I liked her a lot. She had such kind eyes and you could tell that the soul behind those eyes was pure. She's a rare one."

"Yes, she was, you wouldn't be the first to say that."

"Whatever happened to make her so determined to leave in the first place? Do you know it?"

"She was getting married…"

"Awww! That's great news," Miriam said, smiling. She seemed more visibly relaxed right now than she was when she came in earlier on.

There was a knock on the door which Roberts answered, asking whoever it was to come in.

"Good day sir, ma'am. Coffee for Mrs. Aleck," the intern said.

"Oh, thank you!" Miriam replied.

The intern sent the cup of coffee down in front of her and departed immediately. Roberts leaned back, watching, and waiting quietly while Miriam helped herself with the hot cup of coffee before her. He spoke after she had taken the first sip and leaned back into her seat.

"Are you ready to get to business now, Mrs. Aleck?"

"Yes, let's get started."

"Alright, as you said, Justin would want to drag this out and prolong the process unnecessarily so I'll advise that we file for a temporary court order which would mandate him to pay child support and take care of other financial responsibilities while the divorce is being processed, plus you also get to request for child custody while the process is still panning out."

"Okay! And when do we do that?"

"The early the better so I'll have that handled as soon as we're done with this meeting."

"Sounds good to me, Roberts."

"Now, I want you to think carefully about this, is there anything you know or you can remember that Justin is likely to bring up in court and use as a strong case against you."

"Well, aside from working late into the night sometimes and having to run night shifts at the hospital, I can't think of anything else. I've been a great mom to my son. Heck, I've been a better parent than Justin can even dream of becoming."

"Asides that, you can't come up with anything else?"

"Not at all, nothing comes to mind right now. Are you writing this down or…" she looked around the room. "Because I do not see a paper and pen or any secretary jotting down stuff?"

Roberts chuckled, "That's fine Miriam, the session is being recorded. It's easier and more efficient that way."

"I agree," she said. "Anything else?"

"Yes. For the house. How do you both split bills? Mortgages? Debts? Or any other financial obligations."

Miriam's expression changed visibly to that of annoyance; "It's simple," she says. "I pay most of the bills and when I'm handicapped to pay or when it's Justin's time to take responsibility, he comes up with a crappy story about forgetting or something silly of that sort."

"Do you have evidence to back this up?" Robert asked.

"I sure do, some of the receipts are in a folder in which I keep all such documents at home. The rest of the time I do online transactions so I should be able to pull up a receipt from that."

Roberts nodded his head in agreement and continued with his questioning. "Has he ever physically assaulted you?"

Miriam was quiet for such a long time that he thought she was not going to answer. She sat still, staring past him to the glass walls covering the entire conference room. He could tell from the look on her face that she wasn't looking at anything in particular and that her mind was probably traveling a thousand miles in a thousand different directions. He stretched his hand to touch her but withdrew thinking it might startle her, so he used his words instead.

"Miriam…" he called, speaking calming and soothingly. "It's okay. He's not here now, you can open up. Remember you need to not hold back any vital information if you want us to get our case right. We're a team, no blindsiding yeah?"

She drew in a long breath before she answered and said "Yes". Her voice was low and throaty like she was trying to hold back tears.

Roberts gave her a minute to relax and get herself together. "If you want, we could finish this later."

"No…! No…! Please go on, I'm… I'm okay!" she said and plastered a wet smile on her face to convince him that she was.

He held out a handkerchief to her. "Thank you," she said as she took it and wiped her face.

"Let's finish this," she said.

"Do you perhaps want a glass of water?"

"Oh please, do not bother. I'm fine. Now, what were you saying…?"

Roberts looked at her again, like he wanted to be sure she was really okay and she wasn't just saying it.

"Who's filing for divorce?"

"For some reason, he hasn't served me any papers but I know it's imminent. The only reasonable explanation therefore would be that he wants me to file for the divorce."

Roberts smiled, "Not to worry Miriam, you'll be fine. We'll get the divorce papers to him by tomorrow, that…" he paused to look at her, "That, is going to put a start to this entire process. Are you ready?"

"I guess I am, let's just rip off the band-aid and be done with it."

"What bargain are you driving? What do you want to get out of the settlement?"

"Custody of my son, full custody if that's possible. I do not want to toss him around like baseball, and child's support for him; paid consistently and I'm good. He can keep the house and the mortgage debt on it."

"You have certainly thought this through."

"I most definitely have, I have to be proactive in my own way, it's the least I can do."

Robert rose to his feet, prompting Miriam to also stand, "Ma'am, we've come to the end of today's session. As much as I can, I'll try to minimize any direct contact with you, I'll handle all his requests and get back to you on them."

"I don't know what to say, Roberts, thank you so much. Really, I..." she took both his hands in hers, staring directly into his eyes, and said, "I owe you. Thanks a lot."

"Will free checkups for a month cut it?" Roberts asked playfully, which caused her to laugh.

"That's the first time you've done that today," he said.

"Done what?" Miriam asked, genuinely confused.

"Laughed. It's the first time you laughed. It has a nice ring to it. You should do that more often, especially around your son."

Miriam blushed slightly and said to her finally 'Thank you'. They shook hands and Roberts walked her downstairs to her car before returning back to his office.

* * *

"Viyon, go sit your ass down. I don't know what's gotten into you. I let you keep that up and there'd be no one to play in the championship; you'd have sent every last one of them right to the hospital."

Viyon looked around the court at the players groaning on the floor. There were three of them who happened to have come too close to him during the practice. He hit two of them on the ankle while trying to dribble the ball past them, then he accidentally hit the third in his chest with his elbow; causing him to topple backward and land on the pile of the two already injured players on the court.

Without saying a word to the Coach or anybody else, he walked across the hall to the spectator's stand where his bag was lying, picked it up, slung it over his back, and walked out of the court. For some reason, Coach Bucky saw that and said nothing. He probably felt that Viyon needed space.

Jared tried to go after him as he bwas leaving but the coach called him back. "Leave him alone, give him some time," Coach said.

Practice ended five minutes later, owing major to the fact that four of the coach's best players were indisposed. Three of them have been put in that state by the fourth person. The practice was rescheduled to be held two days later to give the injured players some time to heal.

The moment Coach blew the final whistle to signal the end of the practice, Jared picked up his gear and ran straight out of the gym. As he walked, he took out his phone and dialed Viyon. He heard the sound of Viyon's phone ringing around the corner and traced it to the boy's locker room.

Viyon was sitting on the floor with his head bent between his legs when Jared came in. If he heard footsteps or any other sound to indicate the presence of someone else in the room with him, he did not show it. He just sat there, in that posture, unmoving.

"Viyon…" Jared called as he approached slowly. "Hey bro, are you okay?"

There was no response from him, Jared waited for a minute before coming to sit on the bench closest to him, trying as much as he could to keep the physical contact to a minimal.

"It's the alright man. I cannot say that I completely understand how you're feeling right now or what you're dealing with, but I'm going to be here man. I'll be right here with you; I am not moving an inch from here and I mean that literally… you know… like for real."

There was still no response and they both sat still in silence for another minute until Jared caved in and spoke.

"Err... Viyon? I don't mean to break your meditation or ruin the moment or anything like that, but I just... I wanted to know... like... how long is this gonna take? You know... so that I can brace myself mentally. Because I already gave my word, that I was going to stay with you... and..., you know what man? Don't worry about it, take your time. Connect to the universe, I'll wait for it."

"Oh, for the love of flipping French fries and marshmallows, you could not stay quiet for 45 seconds?"

"Was it forty-five seconds? It definitely felt like it was longer. I'm sure it was about five minutes; it was definitely up to five minutes."

"Forget it, bro," he said as he rose to his feet. "Thank you," he clasped his hand on Jared's back and walked out of the locker room. He was a few steps away from the door before he turned and saw Jared still standing at the spot where he left him earlier. "Are you coming?"

"Yeah sure, I sit here for 45 seconds waiting for you, and when you get up what do you do? You walk out the door and bid me farewell, that's what."

Viyon continued towards the door without a second glance in Jared's direction. Immediately, Jared grabbed his backpack and ran after him, "Hey! Viyon, wait up bro."

He got to Viyon then tossed the car keys to him, "You drive, I need some time to catch my breath."

"My parents are in court fighting over who gets custody of what. It's pretty messed up, mom comes back from the court every day feeling worse than she did the previous time and it's killing me because I cannot do anything to help," he said after they were seated in the car.

Jared sat still and quiet for a long while, unsure of what to say to ease the stress of the moment, he simply reached over to the driver's seat of the car and pulled him into a warm hug.

"When did you become touchy-feely?"

"Shut up man! You ruined the moment," Jared signaled him to move over so that they can switch places, he moves across the seat to the driver's side while Viyon opened the door and walked over to the spot that Jared just vacated.

"What do you say we stop by at my house first? I think a glass of warm milk and cookies would help make you feel better," Jared said before starting the car.

"Thanks, but I'm not a good company at this time. Does your mom know about divorce?" Viyon asked.

"She does, but I didn't say a word to her. Trust me. Have you spoken to Amanda? She came by the restaurant looking for you."

"I don't want her to see me like this, I don't..." he paused. "I can't face her just yet. I'm very unstable right now. I feel like I might say something stupid or do something that's gonna make her hate me."

"Keep ignoring her and she's definitely gonna hate you. I don't know why, but she's really into you."

* * *

"Hey honey, how are you? How was practice?" Miriam asked the moment Viyon walked in the door. Viyon dropped his bag on the sofa, going over to peck his mom on both cheeks before taking the seat opposite her.

He was not expecting her to be at home at that time of the day. It was barely 4 pm in the evening; usually, she'd still be at the hospital attending to a patient or doing any of her medical-related duties. But the divorce turned everything inside out for everyone, including her.

The fact that she was home early meant she took an excuse from work, which means she either went to court or she had a meeting with her lawyer. Whichever the case may be, the only thing Viyon was interested in was to have all these done and over with and for life to resume its usual pattern. Nothing would be the same again definitely, but they would finally be able to put this behind them and move on.

"Practice was fine," he lied. The last thing he wanted was to have her worry about him or his mental health or how he was coping in school.

"That's good to know, it ended quite early today, that's unusual. What happened?"

Viyon was spared the trouble of having to tell another lie when the phone rang. She had probably been expecting the call because she stood immediately to get it. "Honey, why don't you take your bag upstairs and get changed? I'll get started at dinner, you can help me when you come back down," she said and pecked him on the head.

"*... And that's my cue,*" Viyon thought. "*She wants to have a private talk.*"

"Can I go for a walk? I want to practice a little bit," Jared asked. If Miriam thought it was weird that he would want to practice after having just returned from the same practice, she didn't say anything about it.

She was already on the call, so she nodded her response and he dashed out, but before he left though; he heard her ask the caller, "How long do we have?". He did not hear the response, but the look on her face pretty much told him what he needed to know. Whatever that was, it wasn't a good one.

He moved away quietly, climbed the stairs up to his room, got changed, and was out of the house within a minute.

Viyon got back about an hour thirty minutes later and came in through the side door. His mom was still in the kitchen when he returned. The soup was still simmering in the pot, which meant she was just getting started with dinner.

"Hey mom, your call ended late?"

"How'd you know that?"

"For one, you're just getting started with dinner."

"Oh," she smiled and looked around the kitchen like she was just seeing all of it for the first time, her face took on a sad expression as she looked. She looked away quickly, hiding her face in a plate cabinet in the pretense of looking for silverware.

Viyon could tell right away that something was wrong. First off, she started dinner late, which is unusual for her. Next, she's making chicken curry soup and apple pie as dessert, after having had such a stressful day, it is the norm for her to order pizza or make a simple meal, not go all out and make a feast. But he sensed she needed time to get herself together before she told him what was happening, so he respected her wishes and did not try to pry it out of her.

"What do I help you with? What do you need me to do?"

"I'm good here as it is, please set the table."

"Wow!" Viyon said with a tone of surprise in his voice.

Miriam looked over her shoulder at him and said; "I know… don't ask any questions and just do it please."

"Viyon…!" she called after him. "Set the table for two. It's just us both."

"I wasn't expecting anyone," Viyon said quietly but loud enough for her to hear. Miriam ignored what he said and continued with her cooking.

Dinner was ready a few minutes later and Viyon helped her move the food to the dining room. After dinner, Miriam gave Viyon an update on the divorce process. The negotiations have been concluded, Miriam gets full custody of the child, while her ex-husband gets the house and the mortgage debt on it. She had been on a call with him earlier on and they had decided that she would get until the end of the week to move out.

"So, we have to move," was all Viyon said when she was done.

"Yes honey, we have to… I know you need some time to take this all in and I understand, everything is happening so fast but we'll be fine…"

"I'll start packing."

"What?!" Miriam asked, taken aback by his sudden reaction. "We still have a full week honey."

Viyon had left the table and was already taking the steps to his room, two at a time. Tired and at a loss for what to do, Miriam slumped back in the chair, placing her head in between both hands while massaging her temple with her fingers. She heard Viyon slam the door to his room and sighed lazily.

She had imagined the whole scene differently when it played out in her head; she knew how much this town and its people meant to Viyon and she hates that she has to pull him out and have them relocate 100 miles away but she would rather this than have Justin gain custody of him.

Justin had put up such strong resistance, using her work schedule as major evidence against her. In the end, Roberts suggested that they settle out of court. He presented Justin with full possession of their current house in exchange for Miriam having full custody of the child. Miriam mentioned that he would have to pay off the mortgage debt on the house but never said how much it was. Justin agreed on the terms that he did not have to alimony or child support for a year, which Miriam agreed to without a fight.

An agreement was reached and the contracts signed to seal the deal. Miriam was overjoyed that she got custody of her son and that she wasn't bothered about anything else. The problem came when she realized she was taking him away from everything he had ever known and loved and that she would have to be the one to tell him.

The ingenious idea to make an elaborate dinner came to her as a way of trying to create a smooth atmosphere so that she could ease into the moment slowly and break the news to him. The plan blew up before dinner. He was on to her the minute he came into the kitchen and saw the preparations for the meal. All she could do was tide along and rip off the Band-Aid at an opportunity time; which she had and he had not taken the pain too well.

"I'm sorry love," Miriam whispered into the air. "I did it for you."

* * *

In his room, Viyon took out a suitcase and started stuffing his things into them, he filled the bag to its maximum and tried to zip it but the zipper got stuck. Angry and frustrated, he dumped the bag back on the bed. With a loud grunt, he pulled the bed sheet off the bed, tossing things around the room.

Miriam heard the noise coming from his room and thought to check it out but decided against it. She would give him time to deal with his emotions. A thought occurred to her and she picked up her phone and put a call through to Jared's mom.

"Hello, Cheryl it's Miriam."

"Oh hello, Miriam… How are you doing? How's the whole process going?"

"It's been concluded, thanks for the concern dear. Can I ask if Jared is home? I'd like him to come over, Viyon's having an episode."

"Oh dear...," Cheryl said in a teary voice. "It's awful what Justin is making you go through, everything is gonna be alright, you'll be fine. I'm positive about that. If you need anything, Miriam, anything at all, you know you can just call." She moved the receiver aside and covered it with one hand before she called for Jared to come down. "Jared...!" "Howdy bunny?"

Jared stuck his head out of his room and screamed out the hallway at his mom. "You promised not to call me that," he said.

"You have someone on the phone for you," his mom replied.

Jared came down the stairs in a flash, he took the phone from his mom with a suspicious look in his eye, then mouthed "Who is it?" at his mom, which she replied with a shrug.

"Hello?"

"Hello Jared, it's Miriam. I was wondering if you could come over and see Viyon."

"What happened to him? Is he okay?" he asked, his voice tinged with concern.

"He's not physically hurt but he needs a friend. He's..." her voice broke. "He's not taking all these too well. He's locked up in his room as we say."

"I'll be over there soon ma'am," Jared said and ended the call.

Miriam met Jared at the door when he came and ushered him into the house. "He's upstairs in his room," she said when he came in. "Thank you, Jared," Miriam said, grabbing both his hands in hers before he ran up the stairs. She heard Jared knock and state who it was at the door before Viyon opened the door to let him in.

Both boys stayed in the room for a really long time when Miriam fell asleep while waiting. Jared came downstairs much later, tailed by a much calmer Viyon. Viyon covered his mom with a blanket and pecked her cheeks after seeing Jared to the door. It was going to be a long road for them but he had finally decided that they would stand a chance of making it if he worked with her rather than fight her. Together they were a team.

Chapter Eight

Jared pulled up in front of Viyon's new apartment, turned off the ignition, and came out of the car, moving round to the other side of the car to get out some of Viyon's stuff that he left with him before they moved.

The new apartment was a flat on the seventh floor of an apartment building downtown, a major drop down from the nice semidetached bungalow where they used to live before. Jared picked up the box mostly filled with work tools and began the walk into the apartment building, praying earnestly under his breath that the elevators were active and working this time.

Last week when he had helped them move in, they had to use the stairs to move a good number of their properties because the elevator was not working. The guard downstairs had told them that it was a technical fault that would be fixed promptly, he swore that the elevators were in good shape and that this issue was not a common occurrence. Miriam had believed him, but Viyon did not try to hide his skepticism of the story.

He entered the lobby and smiled at the guard sitting at his station to his right, he did not realize he had been holding his breath until he got to the elevators and saw that it was in good shape and was actively being used. He dropped the box down close to his feet so he could free up his hands and put in the number for what floor he was going to. The elevator doors closed and began to slide upwards, Jared leaned back against it and heaved a long sigh. He most definitely had not been looking forward to taking those stairs again.

The elevator beeped when it got to his floor and opened up for him to come out. He picked the box up from the floor and started down the hall to Viyon's new apartment. Unsure of what was the flat number exactly, he tried to retrace his steps from the memory of the last time that he was there. He got to a door on the left wing that looked fairly new in appearance and rang the doorbell.

There was no response and he had started to move away when the door opened and Miriam stuck her head out. "Who's there?"

"Hi ma'am!"

"Hey Jared, please come on in. So good to see you; How are you?"

"I'm doing fine, is Viyon home?"

She closed the door behind him and returned back to the place where she had been sitting. The apartment was crowded, with Miriam trying to fit in some of her furniture from the other house into a much smaller space. When Viyon asked her if that furniture was part of the house deal that his ex-dad-Viyon prefers to call him that-got, she replied and said she bought those ones with her money and she had the receipts that came with it.

Jared held onto the box in his hand a little bit longer for lack of where to put it. The sitting room was a small space and Miriam's bookshelf swallowed up a large portion of it. They had brought with them one long sofa and two twin chairs and those had been arranged in a part of the room. The center table looked like it was going to cave under the weight of the textbooks that Miriam piled on top of it.

"Yes, he's in his room, knock on the door to your left. It wouldn't be hard to find, it's a pretty small place," Miriam said with a half-smile and returned to her reading. Jared had a feeling that he could stand there all day and she would only notice him when she needed to get water to drink or take a toilet break.

He finally decided to put the box down in the corner with the sofa. He would let Viyon know where he dropped it so he could place it properly at a later time. He found himself wondering if they'd have an attic, or a garage space but decided that it would be insensitive to ask and swallowed his curiosity.

"Hey bro," he said when Viyon opened the door. Viyon's room looked worse than the sitting room. Everything was still in the boxes that they came in while they were moving. The only thing that had been erected was his bed, the bed laid bare on the wooden frame. No bedsheet, no bed cover, duvet, nothing. Just a plain mattress. Jared looked from the room to its occupant. Viyon looked like a crap.

"You don't look, good man. Have you ever left this room since I was here? And you look like you've skipped a couple of meals or a lot... what's happening?"

Viyon patted a spot on the bed for him to sit on and retired back to bed, curled up in the same way that was before he got up to open the door. "Nothing's happening man, I'm great."

"Like hell, you're not. If this is great, I do not want to see what 'not great' looks like," he said, making air quotes with two fingers. "Come on, get up and go have a bath," he paused, then said; "Don't look at me like that or ask me how I know, boy you reek. Now off you go, go get cleansed."

Viyon resisted at first, but after several minutes of back and forth argument between himself and Jared, he finally gave in. He took off his clothes and dumped them in a pile at the foot of his bed along with others of its kind that have been lying there since the start of the week.

When Jared asked about the messed-up state of his room, he muttered something about finding order in chaos before walking out of the room to use the bathroom. He reappeared at the doorway later on and threatened Jared, not to 'mess' with his stuff.

He peeked in the sitting room to check up on his mom while going to the bathroom. She was still reclined on the sofa, bent over a couple of different textbooks, studying. Viyon figured that it was her own way of dealing with the change. She never really had a life outside of work and home, occasionally she'd go to church, and sometimes she'd hang out with friends; who were mostly other work colleagues who also did not really have a social life.

These days, however, she was even more reserved than she used to be. The routine was a straight line, Work-home. She did very little else in between. Half the time, when she's home from work, her head is bent over the table trying to study and pass an upcoming examination so she can get them out of this shithole as she calls it. It was the first time Viyon had ever heard his mom swear, and he had felt pretty weird about it.

Hot water was out when Viyon got to the bathroom and he cussed the apartment silently to deny him even this basic need. The bath was a quick one, owing to the lack of warm water. He was out of the bathroom and back into the room in no time.

"Did you get to the bathroom? That was fast. So, I told the manager at the restaurant that you are critically ill and you might not be able to report to work for about a week. I was going to tell him you have cancer or a really critical condition but I realize that the goal is to give you some time away, not get you fired so…"

"Thanks, Jared!" Viyon said, his head was buried in his box while he was trying to get a change of clothes.

"Sure bro, it's nothing. Jones' been asking after you though, says he wants to get some flowers and come see you…"

"What exactly did you tell them," Viyon said. "Why on God's green earth would he want to bring flowers? You did not, by any chance, say it was a funeral, did you?"

Jared's face turned pale as the blood got drained from his face because of the audacity with which Viyon said such a thing. "How can you trivialize such things?"

"What's that? Are you afraid of death?" Viyon asked casually. "Now that's why you should go to church."

"You've gone full time cray-cray. Let's go get something to eat, I'll fill you in on practice on the way."

"… Or we could order for pizza and save ourselves the trouble."

A glance at a corner of the room revealed a stack of pizza boxes, stuffed into a corner; a short answer to how Viyon has been getting his meals. "N-O bro. No way, first you take these to the trash" he pointed at the stack of pizza boxes in the corner "… and change that horrible shirt you have on, it looks like something that came out of my Grandma's attic. Then we'll go out of this room, out of this apartment, into the real world and interact with sane, regular people. Now get dressed."

Viyon must have sensed the seriousness in Jared's tone because he got up and made his way out of the room, he did not change out of the shirt he was wearing however as he strolled past him into the sitting room.

Miriam was still at the same spot where she has been all day, head bent over a thousand and one different textbooks. She glanced up when they came into the sitting room. "Mom, I'm going out for lunch with Jared. I'll be back shortly. Would you like me to get you anything?"

"A glass of milkshake would be fine, thank you," she said. "… And son," Viyon paused in his steps on his way out and turned to face her; "Take your time. Don't be in a hurry to come back, I'll be fine."

He came back to the sofa and kissed her forehead before backing out through the front door, his back was turned against her so he did not see her mouth a 'thank you' to Jared; who nodded in reply.

"You know, if you want, I could come over and pick you up and we'll drive down to school every day. It would save you a lot of trouble since you're all about saving yourself some trouble," Jared said on their elevator ride downstairs.

"Thanks, I'll pass," Viyon replied.

"I'll be here at 7:30 am on Monday, don't you dare be a minute late," he grinned at Viyon. "I was going for that Coach vibe, did you notice? Hey…! Slow down. Snob!" he ran out across the hall to the car parked outside before he caught up with Viyon. "Don't do that ever again, that's wicked."

* * *

The class bell rang to signal the end of the class period and the start of the lunch break. Almost immediately, the class became a beehive of activities. Viyon has been back to school for about a week and those five days of learning have been pure torture to him. He knew it was only a matter of time before someone takes notice and as such he had not been surprised when Coach Bucky, his class teacher, and after-school practice coach, requested to see him during the lunch break.

He figured it was not a pleasant visit or a praiseworthy event. Usually, the Coach announces who did well or excelled in what, right there in the class. If he is calling for a private audience, it's probably because he wants to address a nasty situation, and that calls for concern.

Viyon slipped quietly out of the class to avoid Jared's watchful eyes. He made his way down the hall, coming to stop in front of Bucky's office, then knocked.

"Come in Viyon," Bucky replied from the other side.

Viyon opened the door slowly, moving to stand close to his table, then shut the door after him. He made no effort to hide his tension or keep the curiosity from showing in his face as he stood, waiting for Bucky to be done with the work he had at hand and finally grant him an audience.

"Please have a seat, Mr. Aleck."

"Code red...!!! Code red...!!!" Viyon thought, *"This is quite comfortable, Bucky never addresses me by my first name, or even puts a title before it. Now, this is interesting.*

"You might want to be a little bit gentle with the thinking, I can see your brain wheels going round, keep that up and you'd be cussing the migraine that would result from it, for the rest of the day."

Now, this was the Bucky that Viyon was used to. He relaxed a bit and waited for him to shoot.

"I know you're wondering why I called you to my office. Well I'll tell you right now. I'm sure you'd want me to be straight up yeah?" he paused and waited for Viyon to react before proceeding with the conversation. Viyon nodded in response.

"Good! YOUR GRADES SUCK! What the hell is wrong with you? What's going on? You know you can talk to me. I'm your teacher and I want to help. That's why I'm here. That's why I get paid at least. But if it's a girl problem, don't tell me. I don't want to hear any of it, I've got enough of mine to deal with, come back later if you want to hear about it."

He paused to look at Viyon in the eye, his brows raised in question.

"I'm sorry sir, I don't get your question."

"Is it a girl problem?"

"No sir, it's not."

Bucky heaved a sigh of relief, leaned back in his seat, and asked, "Do you want to talk about it?"

"I'm not comfortable sharing it right now, sir."

"That's okay. But whatever it is, you can handle it. I know that because I've watched you over the years and I've seen you stomp things you didn't even know you could beat. I have complete faith in you, and I will not stand by and watch my star player wither away in agony."

"Thank you, sir."

"That would be all, see you at practice this evening… and Viyon, no pressure, but if you do not get your grades up; you would not be allowed to play in the junior championship. And we both do not want that."

"I understand sir; I'll do better."

Viyon left the office, shut the door, and turned to find Jared standing behind him in the hallway.

"Why I'm not shocked that you're here. How did you know where I would be?" he asked Jared.

"I saw you leave the class immediately the bell rang, and Bucky whispered something to you during the first period. Two plus two and Bam! I have my answer."

Viyon shook his head at him, impressed and grateful to have a friend like him.

"What's happening? Are you in trouble? I did not know what to tell Bucky, every time I thought of what excuse to give I remember you messing around with talks of funerals and I just froze. He's not taking you off the team for missing practices, is he? He can't do that; he needs to hear from you. I'll go talk to him."

Viyon pulled him back with his shirt with one hand to stop him in his tracks. "Take a chill pill, it's none of those things."

"Ooooo… kay?" Jared replied, not satisfied with the answer and still thinking he needs to do something to help.

"Yeah, he was concerned about my grades and wanted to know if I'm okay, basic teacher's concern for a student's welfare."

"Oh! That's good, I guess there would be no need for me to barge into his office now."

"Yeah, that's right. Point exactly."

"Let's go get lunch, I'm starving and Amanda has saved us a spot. Don't you dare? Don't even think, don't blink, don't do anything. The girl's been worried about you, the least you can do is show up. She deserves to see you eat at least. Stop being a sissy and go get her." He paused and thought for a moment then said: "maybe that's a little out of context but you get what I mean."

They got to the cafeteria to find Amanda at a table waiting for them, she waved and smiled when she saw them. Viyon did not react fast enough so Jared nudged him with his elbow, prompting him to smile back in return.

Mrs. Perez was behind the food counter when they went to get their meals. As usual, she filled Viyon's plate and added a little extra to put back that meat on his bones. "Thanks, ma'am," he said, then grabbed the tray and made it for the table; Jared already flanking him.

"Look who's back to camp," Amanda said when he got to the table. "It's been a minute, young man. How are you?"

"I've been better," Viyon said quietly. Amanda looked at him with those soulful compassionate eyes that made him feel like he was going to cry, and he looked away to keep himself from doing just that. His eyes caught Jared's as he turned; shooting sharp daggers at him. "Wrong answer bro. Wrong frigging answer!" he whispered close to Viyon's ears.

Amanda had been saying something about the school's calendar for the rest of the year, which he missed because he had been listening to Jared rebuke him in whispers. He caught the word 'prom' when he regained focus and so his next words were: "Would you go with me to prom?"

Jared was stunned for a minute until he realized that the question had not been directed to him. Activity at the table quietened as everyone waited for Amanda's answer; her face reflected the shock that Jared felt at first, no one had been expecting that and they all needed a minute to deal with it. Finally, she smiled and 'yes'.

Jared was overjoyed; jumping about the place, punching the air with his fist, and whooping intermittently. Viyon sat still, smiling and trying to hide his embarrassment from showing, Amanda blushed excitedly as she watched Jared's display. Jared realized he was causing a nuisance when half of the cafeteria turned to watch him jump around. Someone sent a bun flying from one table in the hall and it landed a smack dab on his face. Viyon got up and apologized for the disturbance, pulling Jared down to his seat as he did, to avoid a confrontation.

The bell went off a few minutes later, signaling the end of the lunch break. In a few seconds, the cafeteria had been emptied of its occupants. Viyon and his friends were the last to leave. As he got up to leave, Amanda came round the corner to where he was and kissed him fully on the lips. Viyon almost passed out from the culture shock he experienced when their lips met. As expected, Jared went into a state of frenzied excitement. He patted Viyon so hard on his back that he almost choked.

When Viyon recovered himself, it was all he could do to walk quietly back to class. He was stunned and excited all at once. He kept smiling to himself, replaying the scenario a thousand times in his mind on his way back to class. Amanda was long gone, as he replayed the image in his head, he thought of a thousand ways in which he should have reciprocated; the things he should have said or the way he should have looked at her and he promised to do that the next time he saw her.

Viyon hitched a ride back home with Jared. Miriam was at home when he got back, no surprise there. She spoke with the matron in charge and asked if her work schedule could be revised for the period and she was obliged. She comes home from work earlier these days and spends her time reading and prepping for her upcoming examination.

"Hey mom," Viyon greeted, going over to peck her cheeks. "How are you doing? You're home early from work today."

"I have a late-night shift; I'll be leaving later that day. How did your day go? You seem quite happy."

Viyon went into the kitchen to pour himself a glass of water then returned back to sit beside his mom and tell her about his day. He told her everything; starting with the not too pleasant meeting he had with Coach Bucky, his lunch at the cafeteria with Jared and Amanda, and his request that she goes to prom with him, conveniently leaving out the part where she kissed him after the lunch break and froze all of his brain cells.

Miriam could tell that there was more to the information he was giving her by the look on his face and she tried to tease it out of him but he wouldn't budge and she let it be.

"What's her name?" Miriam asked.

"I thought I mentioned it already, her name's Amanda."

"I don't think you did, you just lit up and gave a whole sermon about her; how she looked, what she smelled like, how she tasted but you never said anything about what she is called."

Miriam pulled her glasses down the rim of her nose and stared at him over the top of the glasses for dramatic effect. Viyon burst into laughter, spurring her to laugh also and they both did. In those few minutes, they let go of their anxiety and pain, expressing their happiness and joy in the purest form of laughter, bubbling out from a depth within them that has been shut off for a good period.

"I'm just glad to see you so happy and hopeful again, it makes me happy too."

"I know… I've got practice by 4 pm which means I need to sleep and be well-rested before then. Jared is going to come by to pick me up and I don't want to delay him."

"That's okay honey, you want me to wake you up or anything?"

"No mom, I'm fine."

"Alright, I made scrambled eggs and toast. There are ham and cheese too, you can have some whenever you're ready."

"Thank you, you're the best," he said then pecked his mom on the cheeks before getting up to leave.

"Son," Miriam called when he was about to leave and he turned back to look at her, "I'm rooting for you. I'm on your side and don't you ever forget that. I want you to win that junior championship match, bring that trophy back home and get the scholarship to study in one of the best colleges that the state can boast of. Let's do that okay?"

"Okay!" he replied, nodding his head as he said to further prove his affirmation. Jared arrived much later on in the day when Miriam was getting to go for her shift at work and they all left together. He and Viyon went to basketball practice, while Miriam went to the hospital.

* * *

The day of the junior championship event was finally here and the hall was packed full of spectators and supporters; friends and families of the teams. Miriam was in the hall this evening; she had prearranged her shift with a colleague so that she could be at the hall for the match. Seated close to her was Cheryl Rowland, Jared's mom.

"Mirrrrrrrrriam…!" Cheryl drawled. "How nice to see you here today."

"Viyon is playing, it's only natural that I show up. I have not seen him yet though, which one is their team?"

Cheryl pointed at a mascot on the court and said: "That's them; The Griffins."

"Griffins, that's a rather strange name…"

"… You think? There's a prefix to it but I mostly leave that one out. It's kind of a mouthful. Anyways, that's their name so…"

"You showed up."

"Well, Jared's in the team too and he is playing today."

"That's great news…"

"Tell me about it. He's been looking forward to this day for as long as I can remember. Usually, he gets benched, but this time the Coach says he has improved and can play on the court with the rest. I got the camera ready, and he asked me to capture every vital moment. I did not ask him how I'd know one of those when it happened. I just simply brought the camera."

Miriam laughed, "It's their moment, let them have it."

"How have you been honey? Jared gives me updates when he comes to visit. If you want, you could have Viyon come to stay over for a week. It would relieve the stress of having to come all that way to school for the time. Jared would be delighted to have him. They are practically like brothers already. He's a part of the family. It would not be a bother, what do you say?"

"Thanks, Cheryl, I appreciate your thoughtfulness, I really do. Let me give it a thought."

"That's fine, whenever you're ready," Cheryl said, then reached out to squeeze Miriam's hand in between hers.

The announcer came up on the mic to announce the start of the games. The players came out in their distinctive jerseys, ushered in by the school's cheerleading team. The crowd stood up with a loud shout to welcome them, everyone cheering for their team. Viyon walked in with Jared behind him, he searched through the hall and found his mom sitting three rows behind the front row with Mrs. Rowland and waved at them.

The players got in position on the court and the referee blew the whistle to signal the start of the game. There have been previous matches before now with different other schools to determine what team will qualify to play with the Mid-West Griffins here at Mid-West high. Mid-West has the honor of hosting the championship finale as standing winners of the previous year's event.

Viyon was stationed in front of one other player as a power forward to play on the offensive and defensive. Agile and quick enough to move around the court, but also strong enough to rebound and parry strikes.

The game had barely begun, when a small forward player from the opposing team rammed into Viyon, causing him to stumble backward and twist his ankle in the process. The referee called out a foul and sanctioned the other team, but the deed was already done. Viyon sustained an injury to his ankle and could not continue on with the game.

The referee blew the whistle to announce a time out and give Viyon's team a chance to strategize and pick a new player to replace Viyon. Miriam ran down from her spot at the spectator's seat and was beside Viyon in no time to give first aid treatment before he was wheeled out of the court.

Coach Bucky got Stilinski to replace Viyon on the court and the game was back on. Miriam would not leave Viyon's side and refused all of his pleas to get back to the hall and find out what was happening. Viyon stayed in tune with the game through the announcer's comment.

The game ended with the opposing team winning with ten points more than the Griffins. From the comments and the crowd reaction, it was pretty obvious that the game was rigged. Jared came backstage to Viyon when the match was over to vent his annoyance. There were a couple of times when the opposing team played a foul and the coach could have called them out but he said nothing. The odds of the game were no longer in their favor the minute Viyon got incapacitated, which made Jared think that it might have been preplanned.

"This whole thing was planned from the start, I'm ready to bet my college funds that your seeming accident, was a malicious attack. It definitely was." Jared said.

"Calm down bro, we can't throw such accusations around. Lets' all credit this one as a bad game."

"Bad game my ass," Jared said. He uttered a foul word that had everybody around turning back to look at him. "Sorry, I got carried away," he said. Apologizing to everyone and no one in particular.

"Well, would you look at that? At least I'm not the only one sensible enough to be peeved about this whole madness" he pointed to Coach Bucky across the hall, arguing with two young men dressed elegantly but casually in jeans and a T-shirt.

"Who are those guys?" Viyon asked.

"Who cares? What matters is that someone gets the brunt of Bucky's angry outburst and they seem like fair enough candidates. For all we know, they could be coaches of the opposing team. Terminators, every last one of them."

Against himself Viyon laughed at Jared's dramatic outburst. Everything about Jared always has something extra and his outbursts are no exception. He comes up with such pitiful excuses for insults that could almost diffuse the moment and make it seem like he was joking if the situation wasn't so serious. Now it was one of such moments.

Both guys found out who the young men in casual clothing were when Coach Bucky came over to inform Jared that they were scouts for a junior basketball team club and that they would like him to play with their team during the summer break.

Jared turned to Viyon to gauge his reaction and see if he was okay with the news, the Coach followed the direction of his eyes and spoke. "I'm sorry little man, I tried to convince them to let you join the team for the summer, told them you were our star player but they were not buying it. They didn't see you play so they were not convinced, plus your grades are down and they do not want you juggling summer school with practice time and a whole bunch of other things that they were worried about."

"Thanks for the effort Coach, I appreciate it and I'll be fine" turning to Jared he said: "Don't you dare turn down that offer," knowing that Jared was most likely thinking about doing just that. "You go there and make me proud man."

Jared and Stilinski were given the scholarship to study at Mid-West senior, for their last final three years before college. Jared hesitated in breaking the news to Viyon, knowing how much Viyon needed the scholarship and how he was better suited to receiving it than he was. However, the news got to Viyon before he left the premises with his mom.

"I know you're worried about me bro, but I'm fine. I don't want you hiding anything from me or making a rash decision that would stall your progress on my account. I would not forgive myself if you do that. I'm happy for you man, be happy. Be proud of your achievement" Viyon said to him, as they hugged before he got in the car.

"I'll come over by weekend, better get some games and snacks ready. Maybe you'll learn some new tricks this time" he shouted after the car as Miriam drove away.

Chapter Nine

Viyon resumes his senior year at a community high school close to their new apartment. His mom had made arrangements for him to start schooling there during the summer break. She had explained to him that it would be difficult trying to pay the house bills and also manage the huge sum that was his fee at the previous school.

This new environment was strange to Viyon. The students here were more rugged and hardened than at his previous school. Unlike Mid-West where a violation of school rules warrants time in detention or suspension from classes based on the gravity of the offense, here violation of laws was punished strictly by manual labor. The offenders are made to do strict and back-breaking activities as punishment.

He walked into the compound cautiously, trying his best not to look like a Newbie and an easy target; even though the sweat was dripping down his back in columns. He tried his best not to hate his mom but he still did. His mind played tricks on him, telling him that all these, the events happening in his life recently, were his doing and his mom blames him for it. That his mom blames him for his dad leaving, for having to give up their nice and comfy apartment and move into this dumpster where they live currently for not winning the scholarship hence the change of school.

Lost in thought, Viyon let his legs guide him to the principal's office. He has been there a couple of times during the summer for his registration process and could remember the way to his office. The secretary was seated at her station when he got there and she motioned for him to sit and wait while she informed the principal of his arrival.

The secretary was a buxom Spanish woman probably in her late thirties or early forties; she shared this same quality with Mrs. Perez but that was as far as the similarities got. While Mrs. Perez was warm and motherly, this secretary was brash and manly in some way. She was tough and you'd be better off not messing with her. Her eyes held no compassion and it looked at you like it could sense that you were hiding something and it's only a matter of time before you're found out.

"Viyooon?" she called a few minutes later, drawling the 'o' lazily. Viyon looked up, he had been fiddling with his hands but he sat up straight now, staring at her whilst hiding how uncomfortable her gaze made him.

She held his gaze for a couple more seconds then said: "No need to see the principal, Mr. Hart will be with you shortly. He is your class teacher. He will show you to your class and help you settle in." As an afterthought, she said: "You are his headache now" and smiled in such a way that Viyon had shivers down his spine.

Mr. Hart came into the principal's office shortly after. He was of average height, wore a pair of thick round glasses, and had kind, compassionate eyes. "Viyon…" he said brightly. "How nice to finally meet you. How are you?" he did not wait for Viyon to give a reply but continued on either way.

"Are you excited about your first day? I don't expect you to be. I'll shit my pants if it were me, strange environment, strange friends, a strange method of teaching. Probably a whole new planet to you. I understand, you should be settled in, in a few days or weeks. That's all it takes; they all get settled in eventually."

He looked at the secretary for confirmation but she continued her work like she had not heard him, or did not know he was talking to her. Viyon could bet that she heard him but chose to ignore, and he was certain that Mr. Hart knew that too.

"Alright young man, if you follow me right this way, I will introduce you to your class and probably your new friends for the duration of your stay here. I learned you were a star basketball player at your previous school. Nice…! We'll talk about that later, for now, we're here" he drew back and stretched his hand forward for Viyon to go into the class, then he walked in behind him.

The class fell silent the minute they both walked in, Viyon thought it was for his benefit, probably based out of curiosity of whom the new guy was, but he was soon to find out how things work at his new school and how Mr. Hart kept order in his class. For his warm and friendly outlook, Mr. Hart was a strict disciplinarian and he had the student's fear and respect.

"Class, this is our newest member. He is a transfer student from one of the best schools in town, so I hope you all understand that it will take him a while to adapt to the teaching style here. Be nice and help him settle in. I do not want to hear about any of that newbie initiation crap. This is not your candidate. You could wait for the next person, understood?" he asked, looking around at everyone in the class to be sure that he was heard and that they would comply.

"Yes sir" they chorused as one. The system here could be likened to a military setting where everything is rigid and programmed to follow a certain order of execution, including the students. His mom had mentioned that this was a disciplinary institution, kind of like a facility for reorienting and educating young people with a strong will and tendency for crime.

"Okay young man, introduce yourself to the class."

"I'm Viyon Aleck," he said dryly.

The class waited for more information but nothing else was forthcoming and some from the class shouted: "Is that all?"

"… That is all you need to know…" Mr. Hart interjected to discourage the others from calling out things too, "… for now," he added.

"Mr. Aleck, you have ten minutes to settle in and get ready for the day's activity. Classes start at exactly 08:10 and the first subject is History. Get a seat and let your butt get used to the feeling of the seat under you because you'd be there for a while, okay?"

"Okay," Viyon said with a nod, unsure of what he meant by the last statement but affirming his consent either way. As he walked into the class to pick a seat, he noticed someone pulling out a seat for him from the corner of his eyes and head in that direction. He might as well acknowledge the first act of kindness he was receiving since he entered the building that morning. That is aside, Mr. Hart.

Viyon felt he would probably get to like Mr. Hart but did not want to be hasty in making such conclusions. Mr. Hart reminded him of Coach Bucky back at Mid-west high, but he felt the two people to be as different as night and day. Whereas the Coach's threats were mere insults shand jabs to get them to be active, he felt Mr. Hart did not bluff and would most probably carry out any of his threats.

"Hi, I'm the Chu" Viyon took the seat after saying his thanks to his benefactor. He looked at the young man who had pulled out a seat for him. His facial structure had an Asian definition of it; small eyes, round face, defined cheeks, and smooth soft lips. He guessed that he was Chinese, but it was hard to tell though. His accent was clean and clear American, the only feature in his structure to indicate otherwise, was his face. The same face which was staring at him now, awaiting a response.

"Nice to meet you the Chu, I'm Viyon."

"I got that during your brief introduction," Chu stared at him like he had a lot of questions to ask but decided this was not the right time and looked away.

"You looked like you were going to say something," Viyon probed.

"Yeah, but Hart does not encourage side talks in his class. We'll talk later."

"But the class has not even started yet," Viyon said but the Chu had turned and was facing the front of the class, an indication that he was done having that conversation.

Chu was later to become Viyon's friend and confidante in his new school. He would also be the one to show Viyon the ropes on how things worked here, get him into a ton of troubles, and also bail him out of a couple.

Viyon settled into his seat as Mr. Hart had advised, ready to start this new phase of life at this new place. He hadn't spoken to Jared or Amanda since the last time they saw each other at the prom.

Jared left him a ton of messages on his mobile phone and the house phone but he did not reply to any.

At first, it started out as procrastination. He piled up the messages with the promise to reply to them later but ends up not doing so as he feels bad about it. Afterward, he just deleted the messages as they came in without even looking at them; it was supposed to keep him from feeling bad about reading the messages and not replying, but he did not feel better.

Instead, every day, he resented himself more and more, and slowly, he drowned in the sea of anger and hate that was building up around him, resenting everyone for the things happening in his life and hating himself for being a hypocrite who throws blames around at other people. The fact that he was forced into a new environment did not help to alleviate his frustration, if anything, it aggravated it. He pretends to be fine and put up a smile when he is around people, but the minute they are gone, he continues to fight the battle in his head for his sanity.

* * *

Viyon got back home on Friday after completing the first week at the new community school. Miriam was not at home but she left a note informing him of her whereabouts and what time she'd be back, she sends her love through the note and tells him to take care of himself.

Chapter Nine

Miriam has sensed that Viyon has been having some real struggles recently but did not think anything of it. She decided to give him space and hopefully, in time, he will heal. She did not want to come at him and overwhelm him, so she allowed him to deal with it his own way. Hopefully, he will trust her enough to share what's troubling him with her.

Viyon dumped his bag on the couch, crashing back into it with a frustrated shout. He was tired and hungry, and at the end of his rope mentally. The agonizing thoughts that he has been battling with throughout the week came to a crescendo and he got the brilliant idea to end it all.

He staggered into his mom's bedroom, holding his head between both hands to stop the thoughts and the headaches that came with it. He pulled out her dresser drawer, took out her anxiolytics, and overturned the container of pills into his mouth. It was too much to gulp down at once, so he spat it out; went into the kitchen to get a carton of milk, and came back into the room to gulp it down in sections.

He did not feel any pain for a few seconds, then suddenly; gradually, the contractions came. His stomach clasped and unclasped as it tried to fight the overwhelming influx of foreign bodies that were threatening to take it apart. He clenched his stomach with both hands as he rolled on the floor in agony, the pain that he felt from his self-induced accident, a welcomed distraction to the voices that have been plaguing his mind in recent days.

As he lay on the floor struggling with the agonized pain that he felt, he hoped for a blackout. This was not going the way he had envisioned it. He had thought it would be smooth and quick. He would feel slight discomfort and then the darkness would overtake him. Ironically, however, darkness refused to come, his eyes were wide open as he struggled to hold on to life or let go. Fear crept in, and he became frantic. He stretched out his hand to reach the top of the drawer and pulled down the telephone. His mom's number was on a speed dial so he called her.

Viyon could hear the phone ring but it sounded so distant, far away, like it was happening in a dream or another parallel dimension.

"Hello…," Miriam's voice came clear through the other end of the phone.

Hearing his mother's voice helped him hold on to consciousness a little bit longer. He opened his mouth to speak to her and let her know what was happening with him, but his words came out as grunts. He sounded so weak and feeble, and after a while, he stopped trying. He was getting too weak to continue, it felt better to just give in and get swallowed up by the oblivion hanging above him.

"Viyon? Son? Are you okay? Talk to me, what's going on?"

Once again, he tried to say something to her but it came out as a weak lifeless groan. This time, the panic in Miriam's voice was as clear as day. "Viyon... hold on. Please, son, I'll call 911. Son, can you hear me? I'm here, I'm right here. I'm with your son, Okay? You'll be fine."

Miriam's voice floated to Viyon from a faraway place beside him, he held on to the voice, letting it soothe his pains and ease his fears. He smiled with the reassurance that the voice gave him. The last thing he remembered was the rude interruption of his peaceful atmosphere. He heard the sound of the siren; footsteps coming down the hall, a knock on the door and a young man with strong muscular arms lifted him up like he weighed nothing more than a few packs of the chip. There was noise and commotion around him. He heard the man say something about an overdose, and just before he shut his eyes, he saw his mom pushing past the people to get to him, smelt her fragrance, and then, there was nothing.

Viyon woke up with a throbbing headache on the side of his head. He tried to sit up and pull himself out of bed when a sharp pain by his side sent signals flying to his brain, causing him to reclined back on the bed. He opened his eyes then shut them back quickly, flinching at the intrusion of the light on his eyes. He opened them back up again, slowly this time, trying to take in as much of his environment as he could. His entire body felt like a thousand needles were piercing through him all at once, leaving no space for flesh. A quick look down his hands and the rest of his body lying on the bed proved that his feelings were not farfetched from the truth. He tried to remember where he was and how he got here, but his memory was foggy.

His mom stirred in her sleep, a few feet away from him on the extra couch provided in the hospital room. He realized immediately that she had been here for as long as he had been in that bed. "Exactly how long has he been here?" he thought. As hard as he tried, he could not conjure up the memories of what happened to put him in this bed. His entire body felt cramped so, in a bid to get some relief and stretch himself a little, he tried to sit up again, but this time, slowly and deliberately to avoid ticking off the pain in his sides again.

The bed creaked as he struggled to sit up and Miriam stirred in her sleep again. Her eyes caught his figure on the bed and she was awake and beside him in no time.

"Honey, you're awake," she said with a half-smile. Her eyes had bags underneath them, the size of an almond fruit, prove that she has not had much sleep these past few days. Couple with her numerous shifts at work and her other busy schedule, the last thing she needed to be doing now was to lose sleep, and Viyon felt bad for being the one to cause that to happen.

Despite her obvious fatigue, she sounded bright and alert. She was active the minute she noticed that he was no longer asleep. Her nursing and motherly instincts kicked in and she knew what he needed, what he was trying to do before he said it.

"Hold on, let me help you with that," she reached below his bed for a lever, holding the top part of the bed with her hand, she pulled the lever and pushed the bed forward at the same time. She let go when the bed had taken on the position she wanted and it latched back into place immediately.

"There, that's better, right?" she asked.

"Yes, it is, thanks, mom!"

Miriam looked at him with eyes brimming with compassion and sadness, he could tell that a million things were going through her mind, dozens of questions lurking behind her eyes that she wanted to ask and he did not blame her, he had questions too. She drew in a deep breath instead, her eyes still fixed on his body, alert to any sudden movement or reaction, then asked him: "How are you feeling?"

"My whole-body hurts, there's a sharp pain in my side and this throbbing headache feels like it has become a part of me."

"Sorry honey, I'd request for some painkillers from the doctor. Why don't you try and get back to sleep?"

"It feels like that's all I've been doing. How long was I out?"

"You were out for two days' honey, but it's fine. You're fine now and that's what matters most. Thank God! I wouldn't know what to do with myself if I lost you."

"What happened? I've been trying to remember, but my memory is all foggy and it hurts too much. I can't even hear myself think with all the pain going on in my head, so I stop trying to remember."

"Get some rest," she said, patting his forehead gently before placing a kiss on it. "We can talk about that later. I'll go ask the doctor for some pain killer. I'll be right back."

"Excuse me please," Viyon heard his mom talking with someone outside the door, probably a doctor or a nurse. He tried to think of the events that happened two days ago to bring him here. He did not even know what day it was. He assumed that it most has been a sensitive issue to have mom, avoiding talking about it, and running out to get pain killers instead. An excuse which he knew was to help her get away from the room and buy her more time.

All that physical and mental activity made him feel drained and tired and he reclined back to bed again and drifted off to sleep in no time. Miriam returned back to the room with the pain killers to see him soundly asleep again. She pressed the lever below the bed again to return the bed back to its original position, adjusted his cloth around him then kissed his cheeks again before proceeding back to her place on the couch. It was 01:39 am in the morning. If she slept now, she'd be able to get some rest before daylight. She took one more look in his direction to make sure he was okay, before drifting off to sleep.

* * *

Daylight came with increased activity around the room and in the corridor. Viyon could hear footsteps of people walking up and down the corridor; room doors opening and closing, voices in his room talking quietly above his head. He felt a warm hand on his neck and hands and opened his eyes.

"You're awake, good morning Viyon."

Viyon squinted his eyes slightly to try and reduce the light intake and focus on the face dancing above him. The doctor saw that and mistook it for lack of recognition, so she introduced herself.

"I'm Doctor Tara, your mom's colleague. I've been to the house a couple of times."

"I remember your ma'am. I was trying to focus my eyes so I could see you better."

"How are you feeling this morning Viyon?" the words were directed to him but her attention was divided between himself, the logbook in her hand for writing down details about the patient and how their health is progressing, and the nurse standing close to her.

"I'm better now, the nagging headache has stopped and the pain in my side feels a little bit numb."

"That's good. It means the pain killers your mom requested last night were quite effective. We'll keep you here till the end of the day to examine your progress and how fast your recuperation, if you show steady progress till evening, you should be ready to go back home by the end of the day or by morning tomorrow. You'd like that, wouldn't you?"

"Yes, very much, thank you. Have you seen my mom?"

"She'd be here soon, she had to attend to an issue downstairs. There's a button at the side of your bed, if you need anything, press that button, and a nurse will be right here to attend to you."

* * *

Miriam came by later in the day to break the same news to Viyon that the Doctor had already told him in the morning. "Honey, you should be out of here by tomorrow. We'll be back home and you can have your friends come visit."

"Doctor Tara already me that this morning," he said.

"You do not seem very excited about that," she noticed.

"I am, at least I was until you mentioned having my friends come to visit. Those guys are not my friends. I do not have any friends there, and I cannot be the new freak in school that ends up being hospitalized after the first week. They already think I'm a sissy, I can't make them think worse."

It took Miriam a few minutes to understand what he was saying, she had been talking about his friends from Mid-West, not the students at his new school.

"I was talking about Jared and Amanda, honey."

Viyon's expression changed visibly and his face became clouded. He looked away for a minute then turned back to face her and said: "I do not want them to visit either."

The Doctor came back to check up on him later in the evening, Miriam was there this time and they talked; exchanging knowledge with their medical jargons. Doctor Tara finally said they were free to leave later on that evening, or they could stay the night and leave by morning but Viyon insisted that they leave that evening so Miriam got their things packed and moved to her car.

A wheelchair was made available to transport Viyon down to the car, but he turned it down, insisting on walking to the car. Miriam put her hand around his side to support him as they walked downstairs to the car park. He felt light and weak around her. He had not had much to eat since his stay at the hospital and she made a mental note to make him something he liked to spur his appetite to eat.

The drive back to the house was a long one. Miriam drove slowly and carefully below the speed limit to make sure Viyon was comfortable. The fact that he reassured her about a hundred times that he was okay did little to change how she was driving. They got to the apartment building about 30 minutes later, two times what it would have been if Jared or Viyon were driving that distance.

Miriam helped him out of the car into the lobby and the elevator. She put in the number for their floor and let him lean against her as the elevator moved upwards. The elevator dinged when it got to their floor and she helped Viyon out, walked him into their apartment before going back downstairs to get the bags.

Alone in the apartment, Viyon staggered off to his bedroom to go lay down and wait for her to come back up. His mom's room was open when he passed; and he could not help but notice the complete state of chaos. That was very unlike his mom, so he moved closer to get a good look at it, then he saw her empty pill container on the floor; the telephone lying close to the bed, the bed undressed with the blanket hanging out by the side, scattered pills on the floor and it all came back to him.

Viyon leaned against the side of the door to gain balance as flashes of images of the night when he tried to kill himself came flooding back. Gradually, he remembered. He remembered the sensations; the voices, the pain, the fear, the commotion, his mom's face hovering above him before he blanked out and he cried.

Miriam came back upstairs to see him still at that spot, tears running down his face. Worried, she ran to him and helped him move into the room and sit on the bed.

"I tried to kill myself..." he said, sobbing.

Miriam looked at him, her eyes filling up also with tears and compassion. She pulled him into a hug, but he wiggled free. Turning to look at her in the face instead, he asked: "You knew, why didn't you say anything?"

Miriam bowed her head to hide the tears that were already freely rolling down her cheeks. "I did not want to believe that you'd do that. That you would even think of doing that and the psychiatrist I spoke with, said it was better not to rush things or make you feel threatened until we're sure that you're out of that place."

"You're seeing a shrink?"

"Yes, I've been having sessions with her in the past few weeks and they've been very helpful. I booked you up for a couple of sessions too."

"I do not need to see a shrink. I do not want to sit across a table from someone who's bored and have them look at me through their glasses like I'm a parasite being examined."

"Hey, calm down," Miriam said quietly, tenderly. "I know you do not want to see a... what did you call it?"

"A shrink...?"

"A shrink. Yes. But please son, do it for me. I don't know what made you ever think of doing that and you did not talk to me, but I feel like talking to someone with a different face might help you pour out your frustrations and finally get some relief about how you feel."

Viyon was still quiet and Miriam knew she had not convinced him, "Viyon? Please...Try out a session and if you still feel skeptical about it, we'll find another way. But I need you to let it out, talk to someone, anyone. Punch the wall, break some stuff, scream, express yourself, but stop bottling things up inside you. It's okay to cry sometimes son, or show emotions. But please, do not ever try to take your life," she reduced her voice to a whisper and said more to herself than to him "I would not be able to live with myself if I lose you."

"I'll do it. I'll try out a session and if it doesn't work out, at least I tried."

"That's all that I need from you son," she kissed his forehead then helped him to his room. "Get some rest, I'll get started on dinner."

The Chu came by later in the evening to check up on Viyon and Mom persuaded him to stay for dinner. He was dressed in baggy shorts and a tank top. His hair was ruffled and windblown, making mom wonder if he ran down here. The Chu must have caught the strange glances thrown his way because he explained having ridden his bicycle all the way down to their apartment. He called his aunt from their house to inform her of his whereabouts after Miriam finally persuaded him to stay.

"I snuck into Mr. Hart's office to get your residential details. I could have just asked him but I didn't want to draw any attention to you. I figured you'd not want that," Chu said.

"Thanks, man, you know me."

"How are you feeling? I learned you tripped down the stairs, aww," he made a facial imitation of someone in pain and said, "that was a rough man."

Viyon was surprised at the variation of information that Chu had, nobody said anything to him about saying something else to the school and his classmates. He looked at his mom for some sort of explanation but she had her back to him and totally missed it.

"Um... yeah... yeah! I...um... I tripped, and err... fell. I fell down the stairs."

Viyon looked at Chu expecting him to call him out on his lie or press for more information but Chu simply nodded and moved on to another topic. Subconsciously, Jared came to mind. Jared would have spotted his lie from a mile and called him out on it. He picked up his phone to call Jared but decided against it. Jared would be down here in less than the time it takes to fry a plain omelet and his cock and bull story of falling down the stairs would not cut it; He didn't even have an injury to show for it, so he put down his phone.

Dinner was a quick and smooth affair, they ate in companionable silence, occasionally Chu would start up a discussion and mom would chip in a comment here and there but eventually they both get bored and Chu brings up something else to keep the talk going. Mom offered to drop him off after dinner but he declined. After exchanging hugs with Viyon, he was ready to go. He called when he got home to let Viyon know that he was home. Mr. Hart called a few minutes later to ask about his welfare and find out when he was going to resume school. After the call, Miriam informed him that he had to be in school by Monday or risk telling the principal what really happened.

Chapter Ten

"Alright Honey, have a good day. Take care of yourself okay. Call me when you get back home from school," Miriam drew him closer and pecked his nose and his forehead.

"Mooooooooom…!" Viyon groaned. "You are going to give me a reputation for being a mama's boy if you keep kissing me this way in school." He looked around to make sure no one was watching, before coming out of the car.

"Call me okay?" She yelled as she backed the car out of the curb. She had insisted on driving him to school every day for the duration of his convalescence period. They had developed a new routine, one that Viyon was not too happy about. She drives him to school every morning, when he gets back from school at noon, he would call her to let her know he was back and she would send Mrs. Pettigrew over to sit with him till evening time when she would be back from the hospital. They had debated the idea of Mrs. Pettigrew coming over for about thirty minutes until she asked if he would rather that Jared or Amanda came over. He conceded grumpily. Miriam did not understand what happened between himself and

Jared and why Viyon was bent on widening the deep chasm between them that he created in the first place, but the fear of having them around serves her well when the time arises.

Viyon caught a vision of someone running towards him from the corner of his eyes and turned quickly to avoid being bumped into. The student ran past without as much as a nod of acknowledgment or a second glance in his direction. Viyon continued with his walk and his reverie was unbothered. He doesn't have many friends at this school. He had not exactly made it easy for anyone to approach him and start a simple conversation. Frankly speaking, the only friend he had was Chu and that's because Chu is as tenacious in wanting to be his friend as he was discouraging him to be one.

Amanda had called again last time and after ignoring the call the first two times that the phone rang, Miriam decided to take the call. She did a good job of sounding upbeat while dishing out a bowl full of lies to cover up for Viyon. She mentioned that Viyon had just been discharged from the hospital some days back, Amanda must have gasped because Miriam began to reassure her of his well-being, passing it off as nothing serious that he could not beat and be back on his own two feet in no time. Miriam ended the call with a promise to let Viyon know that she called when he woke up and had him return the call when he had been sitting close to her and had heard the entire conversation.

"That's the last time I'm doing that for your young man. You have such amazing friends and you treat them like trash. You should be grateful for these people and treat them better, at least call them and let them know you need some time to get your acts together. I raised up better than this," Miriam said after she ended the call.

Jared called while she was still chastising Viyon for being a terrible friend and he pleaded with her to take the call. It would not exactly tell well if Viyon takes the call when he was supposedly asleep, Miriam knew she had just been blackmailed, she shot daggers at him with her eyes then mouthed "last time" before she took the call. Amanda had informed Jared about Viyon's medical condition and he called to be sure he was okay. Miriam reassured him that Viyon was fine, then he asked her if Viyon was avoiding him and she replied that he would have to ask Viyon that for himself. After the call, Miriam asked Viyon to call them both back and stop being a shitty friend.

"You look like a zombie from resident evil. Slow, emotionless, and all drag... drag... drag." Chu imitated what Viyon must have looked like walking down the hall with such a dull expression on his face, lost in thought.

"Good to see you too man," he replied dully.

"What? That's it? That was supposed to brighten you up, a smile at least."

When Viyon said nothing else and continued walking down towards their classroom, Chu took the hint and followed behind still chattering. "My aunt sent you some balms. She said it would soothe your muscles and help relieve the tensions because you walk around like you so stressed and you got the world on your shoulders" Chu did not wait for Viyon to ask to see the balms, he brought them out of his bag and transferred them straight into Viyon's backpack. "She will be heartbroken if you turn down her gift and I can't be the one to lie to her," he explained after he had done what he wanted to.

"I'm glad you're back man, are you fully recovered? We've got P.E today and those sessions are just bloody insane. I would not hesitate to pass it up. I just need to tell Mr. Hart I'm still recuperating and he'll write a note to the gym teacher. What do you say?"

"Thank I'm good" they were in class now and Viyon dropped his bag and settled into his seat. Chu put his bag down but stood close to Viyon's table, staring at him like he was expecting him to do something. Viyon looked up at him and asked, "What?" Chu nodded towards the rest of the class and Viyon followed the movement of his head. It was then he realized that the classroom was empty except for the two of them.

"Where's everybody else?" he asked, with the slightest hint of emotion.

"Down at the gym" Chu replied, looking pointedly at him.

"Oh!" Viyon said as he realized why Chu must have said those things to him a few minutes ago. His mom's words came back to him and he relaxed a little. "I'm sorry," he said. "I've been a shitty friend, haven't I?"

"Yup, you have… the shittiest of them all," Chu replied, which made Viyon smile.

"I'll try to act more human from this point on…" Chu leaned in for a hug but Viyon pushed him back with one hand. "Don't, get all touchy-feely already. Gross!" he punched him in the stomach instead, and Chu retaliated. The duo struggled with each other, trying to knock out the other when the sound of someone clearing his throat at the door interrupted their moment.

"Viyon!" Mr. Hart said brightly. "Good to have you back, not for long though judging by the fact that your friend here is trying to choke you and send you right back to the ER." He looked at Chu and said: "You're late for gym class" as an afterthought he added, "You have five minutes, both of you."

Both guys ran out of the class, changed into sportswear, and were at the gym in exactly five minutes. Chu passed out on the floor the moment he stepped into the gym and laid there, trying to catch his breath. When he had put himself together and could catch his breath long enough to speak, he sorts out Viyon and was going to take permission from the coach on his behalf but saw him already in formation, doing warm-ups.

"Seriously dude, you didn't even break a sweat. What are you?"

"Hey you," the coach shouted at Chu across the hall, "Less chitty chat and more working out okay?"

"Got it, coach," Chu said, he moved a few inches away from Viyon to do his warm-ups but made sure Viyon was still in view. The warm-up lasted five minutes, after which the coach blew the whistle to signal the end. He asked them to split into two groups, with two captains. Chu and Viyon ended up in the same group against a band of bigger, stronger boys. The ladies were also separated into groups.

"I want a fair game. Put the ball through the net, the team with the highest baskets wins. While you're at it, I'm going to be looking out for speed, team spirit, and agility. If I find these qualities in you, you make the team and you get to play for the school this season, any form of violence, cheating, or aggression and it's bye-bye for this season. Understood?"

The boys chorused a "yes sir" and the coach blew the whistle to get them to take the right formation. Instinctively, Viyon took on space in front as the power forward, his team captain did not say anything about it so he remained there. The first few minutes of the game were rough and embarrassing for his team. Chu got hit with a ball in his forehead twice, which caused the other team to erupt in laughter and throw jabs at them. The other team was in the lead with six baskets while his team had only three, he had scored one and the team captain had two. Viyon waited patiently for the coach to say something, issue a card or call out a foul, but he said nothing; concentrating instead on fishing out the traits he mentioned earlier on.

Viyon decided that you create your own rules for the game, having used the first twenty minutes to figure out the opponent he activated play mode. Chu got caught with a ball to his stomach this time and fell to the ground, when the ball got passed to Viyon he aimed for the person who hit Chu earlier and sent the ball flying at him. The ball hit him in the groin and he collapsed to the floor in pain, clutching his organ with both hands. The hall fell silent for a second. The opposing team saw what happened and did not appreciate being the object of the joke. Viyon now had a target on his back. He dribbled through the mass of offenders coming at him and scored a basket against them. His team erupted in a loud cheer, Chu joined in too, having recovered slightly from his freak accident. The score lifted their spirit and the game tide turned in their favor.

The game was a tie now, each team had six baskets to their name, it was less than two minutes to the end of the match, the team to score a basket at this point, wins the game. The ball was with Viyon, he was dribbling between players to get close enough to the basket to do a slam dunk when someone attacked from behind, his brain replayed a déjà vu moment of when this happened at the junior championship and by reflex, he used his elbow to hit the attacker in the stomach, while moving quickly at the same time to avoid being a kick in his shin. The attacker drew back in pain and Viyon jumped to score the final and winning goal against them. The coach blew the whistle to signal the end of the match and the hall became a madhouse. Viyon's team shouted excitedly, whistling and carrying him up on their shoulder to celebrate their victory.

"That's enough, gather round everyone." The students assembled in the middle of the gym, Viyon's teammates were still giggly and excited, the win came as a shock to everyone, them especially. "That was an interesting match," the coach said. "... And it's quite clear to all that Rufus' team won. Congratulations guys, you have an athletic genius on your team." The team cheered again, each member of the team reaching out their hand to clasp Viyon on the back.

He listed the name of the team members to go ahead and make up the school's team for the season. After giving a couple of minor announcements, he ended the class. The coach made me leave the gym but then turned back halfway through. "Viyon, please see me in my office during lunch break," he said and left.

"Whaaaaaaaat!!! That was the most amazing thing I've seen all year," Chu said. Chu kept on talking about the match, he narrated a somewhat exaggerated version of what actually happened back to Viyon, then suddenly stopped talking. He moved closer to Viyon and said: "Don't look but you have eyes on you, 4, O clock." Viyon moved his head slightly to see what Chu was talking about but Chu pinched him hard and said: "I just told you not to look, what part of that do you not get? Viyon...? Viyon keeps walking. Don't do it." Viyon let go of Chu and turned in the direction that he indicated, he had a daring look on his face that had Chu worried, the guys advanced towards them and Viyon stood, unrelenting, waiting for them to approach. Mr. Hart came around the corner and the group dispersed, ending what would have been a showdown before it even started. Viyon did not miss the look on the guy's face as they left, clearly, this was not over yet. The showdown would happen later. Hopefully, Hart will not be present and they can settle the scores.

Chu begged Viyon to walk away. Obviously, he had been in a rough spot with these guys and did not repeat. "I hate guys like them," Viyon said.

"Tell me about it," Chu replied.

"You two again, is this becoming a habit? You've got chemistry now and the lab is that way," Mr. Hart said, pointing in the direction of the laboratory.

Chu and Viyon scrambled off to the lab. The seats were already full except for two seats at the back of the class which they occupied immediately. The rest of the day went smoothly, a normal, regular everyday school routine. Mr. Hart announced later on to the class that they would be sitting for their G.E.D at the end of the month. He offered to give extra lessons to anyone struggling with any of the subjects and needed help. He asked them to sign up after class at his desk, a couple of students indicated interest and were signed up.

"Viyon," Mr. Hart called. "I made this arrangement specifically with you in mind, seeing as you have missed a whole lot of school activities and lessons this session, I would have expected that you sign, instead you sit put, brimming with confidence. The offer is still open, sign up anytime."

Chu gave Viyon a pleading look for him to go and pen down his name while Hart is still in class, but Viyon ignored the look, pretending not to have seen it. The bell rang to signal the end of the class and the class emptied almost immediately. The news of what happened at the gym earlier on had spread throughout the school and people paused in their steps to nod at Viyon, a couple of them said Hi, and Viyon replied back.

Viyon noticed the guys that they had played against approaching from behind and would have said something to Chu but Chu had gone ahead of him, he was enjoying the attention that came with walking with the new star athlete and basked in it. One of the guys reached him before Viyon could and punched him in the stomach, Chu had not been expecting that so he had no time to dodge it, he staggered slightly, clutching his stomach with his hands. Viyon ran to his side and helped him up. From the side of his eyes he saw two others advancing towards them. He thought fast and acted quickly. He picked up his backpack and hurled at the guy on his left, dodging a punch. He picked up Chu's bag and sent it flying at the other guy, he had anticipated that so he hit the bag away with his hand and charged at Viyon. Viyon used his opponent's blind rage against him, he waited until he was close enough then slid under him and kicked him from behind, the opponent ran straight into the locker, the kick from behind amplifying the forward charge. One of the students had escaped when the fight was starting out and returned with a teacher. Of course, the student was smart enough not to be seen or it would have spelled trouble for him.

"All of you, in my office, now."

Each person picked themselves up, put up a bold face, and walked haughtily behind the teacher to his office. Viyon tried to think up possible explanations for his actions but could not come up with anything, he decided that whatever story he was going to tell had to be in sync with Chu's version and since both of them are so far away, under close surveillance, they couldn't band together now and cook up a story. Eventually, the cover-up story was not needed as nobody asked anything about what happened. Whoever tipped off the teacher about the fight, had probably also mentioned how it started and who initiated it. The teacher seemed to be in the know when he addressed the conflict and meted out punishments to both parties. Everyone got suspended, Viyon and Chu for three whole days, the team opposing side for a week.

After they left the office, Viyon sighed deeply. Glad that he had not been asked to bring his mother to school. If that happened, he would have been caught and Miriam would be further distraught that her son was becoming a rascal. When he voiced the reason for his happiness to Chu, Chu told him not tp rejoice yet. The school might call their parents to inform them of the suspension, and in the case that it doesn't happen, they would still have to find a way to inform their parents that they have been suspended. Viyon especially, seeing as Miriam insists on dropping him off at school every morning. Their concerns were unnecessary as neither of the above happened. Miriam's car had a fault and had to be taken to the mechanic, so she couldn't drive Viyon to school during that period.

Chapter Ten

* * *

On the first day of his suspension, Viyon got dressed and ready for school so that Miriam didn't suspect anything. After that, he was fully dressed and prepared; lunch packed, books and all, he goes to sit in the sitting room, legs crossed, nibbling on a sandwich. Miriam comes to the sitting room to find him reclining comfortably on the couch.

"Did I miss something?" she asked.

"What?" Viyon asked, with a mouthful of peanut butter sandwich.

"Young man, you should be on your way to the bus stop to board the bus to school."

"Oh... I'm waiting for Chu; he is my new guardian angel." Viyon gave a further explanation to dissipate the confused look on her face. "Chu insists on riding me... taking me to school. I told him about your car trouble."

"Alright honey, I have to run along now or I'm going to be late. Call me when you get back from school okay?" she pecks on the cheek before leaving. Chu came by later in the day and they both walked out of the apartment building together to give the impression that they were leaving for school. They would later sneak in through the back, up to the apartment where they would play video games and watch movies till they pass out. This became their routine for the duration of their suspension.

Occasionally they almost had slip-ups. One time before noon, while they were playing games, the telephone rang, and Viyon rushed to take it, he realized himself after he had answered and inflected his voice to sound like the voice mail machine. They had a good laugh after he dropped the call. The next time, Mrs. Pettigrew thought she heard some noise coming from their apartment and to the best of her knowledge, Viyon was in school and his mom had gone to work. She knocked on the door and they suddenly went still using sign language, they signaled each other to turn off the T.V or put out the light, basically do everything to make the house seem uninhabited. Mrs. Pettigrew listened from outside the door, thinking that it was probably a thief and the Alecks were being burgled, she threatened to call the police. Out of options and afraid that Mrs. Pettigrew might carry out her threat, Viyon opened the door.

"Hello ma," he coughed and tried to look sick to complete his act. "I thought I heard you knock."

Mrs. Pettigrew's brave face quickly became one of concern and compassion. She was at his side immediately. "My boy," she says, "What's wrong?"

"I feel sick and I want to rest a little. I already told my mum so you don't have to bother, Oh and I have company so there is no need to be afraid that I'm alone and I could get into something crazy. There's none of that for me. Just rest."

Mrs. Pettigrew bought the story and was out of their hair, but she didn't stay out of their hair for long. Every few minutes, she'd come by to check up on him with some fruits or a bowl of soup or drop some suggestions on how much water he should take, the room temperature, amongst others. Viyon was overjoyed when his mom got back from work as that would mean the end of Mrs. Pettigrew's concern visits. Fortunately, also, the end of his and Chu's suspension from school. Somehow, they managed to handle the situation without letting both parents or guardians know about it.

Viyon helped out with the dinner preparations. If mom was surprised to find Chu at home when she got home, she didn't say anything about it. It was payday, so mom treated them to a whole banquet. It was a feast for royalty. It was a weekend so they were allowed to stay up late and watch TV. Viyon almost had a heart attack when his mom came into the sitting room to announce that someone from their school called. The boys paused in their activity and exchanged looks with each other. Perhaps they had not been very smooth with their cover-ups and a loose end was coming to bite them now.

"His name's Mr. Hart said your class teacher."

Unable to bring himself to voice out, he nods in reply, his heart pounding hard against his chest. Beside him Chu contemplated letting the cat out of the bag by himself. Maybe that way she would not be as annoyed as she would be. It was a stupid thought but he needed to do something. As if Viyon could read Chu's thoughts and guessed what he was going to do, he punched him to stay still.

"He called to inform me about G.E.D examination that you are to take at the end of the month, and he says since you've missed so many of your classes, he would have advised that you stay back after school to join the makeup classes he is having with other students."

Viyon and Chu sighed deeply, relieved that they had somehow managed to escape. Miriam continued: "I don't know why he would say you missed 40% of school activity, that's a lot. I mean asides from the fact that you resumed a week late, and the week when you were hospitalized, you haven't happened to miss school again have you?"

It was a rhetorical question and they knew that because Miriam did not wait to get an answer but continued her pacing and pondering, but still, they were uncomfortable that the question hit so close to home.

"That aside, the most important factor right now is for you to join the makeup classes and be aptly prepared to sit for the G.E.D. He said the classes have already begun and I wonder how you didn't know that, but you can join in on Monday. The change in your schedule wouldn't be that much. You will only stay back after school for an hour every day and on weekends, you spend four hours. That's fair enough, don't you think?" she asked. This time it was not rhetorical as she waited for him to reply. Viyon swallowed, then nodded in response.

"Good. He said he'll see you on Monday. Now you both should not stay up so late. We're going to church tomorrow."

"Whaaaaaaaaaaaaaaat?" Viyon exclaimed.

"You heard me right, see you in the morning."

"But tomorrow is not even Sunday. It's Saturday, today is Friday, remember?"

"Oh...!" she paused. "Well... sleep tight, wake up early, but we're still going to church on Sunday," she winked at him at the door before turning the corner to her room.

When they were sure that she was out of sight, Chu leaned close to Viyon and asked: "Your mom's religious?"

"Um... once in a while," he replied.

Chu looked like he was going to say more but his favorite character in the movie was in a dilemma, the suspense in the movie was palpable so much so that Chu lost track of what he was going to say, to capture every moment of what was going to happen next. The boys slept late that night, curled up against each other on the couch. Miriam came out later in the night to use the bathroom and smiled at the sight of the two musketeers. She got a blanket from Viyon's room and covered them with it.

* * *

Viyon returned back to school on Monday with mixed feelings. On the one hand, he was getting tired of the drama and lies that came with having to stay at home because of the suspension; on the other hand, he would give anything to be anywhere else but here. It was bright and sunny, if he were to judge by the weather or any of those weird astrological readings that people do, he would say this was going to be a good day. Chu had the flu and could not come to school. It sounded like he was joking when he called Viyon to tell him that he wouldn't be in school due to the illness.

Mr. Hart seemed happy to see him, too happy if you asked Viyon. "Welcome back, hopefully, you will stay longer." Viyon thought the statement seemed suspicious or sarcastic in a way but decided it's best not to give it any serious thought. "Thank you, sir!"

"Where's your other half?"

Viyon knew he was asking after Chu but wanted to draw out the conversation longer so he acted ignorantly. "I'm sorry sir, but I do not understand what you mean."

Mr. Hart looked at him long and hard as if trying to decipher whether or not he was being serious or if he was just messing around, in the end, he simply said: "Never mind. I'll see you after school hours for makeup classes. He left without another word.

Somehow Viyon knew he no longer had a say in deciding to join the class or not, so he saved himself from the stress of arguing. His initial prediction of how his day was going to go based on his weather astrological readings turned out to be a total flop. The day dragged on forever, mostly because Chu was not around to create a diversion for him during the long class hours, lunch break was a tedious affair and just when he thought he could finally escape it all, Mr. Hart called them together to start the makeup classes.

The class was not as bad as Viyon thought it would be, he had expected that he would end up in the company of some not so intelligent students, or on the flip side, be the only non-nerd in a sea full of nerds. Mr. Hart took his time to explain the basic intricacies of the subjects that they were going to write during the GED. Those subjects were the focus of their extra-curricular activities. The class ended exactly an hour later, so Viyon did not have to stress Mr. Hart eating into an extra time. He found himself enjoying the lessons and looking forward to the next one.

The next couple of weeks passed in a blur of activities. A significant part of the blur was the makeup classes. Every day after school for the past few weeks, Viyon stayed back to join in the after-school class. Chu was fully recovered and resumed school, he joined the makeup class and with a little bit of help from Viyon was able to get right back on track.

Viyon felt like his life was striking a balance again. It had started to have a steady rhythm to it that he enjoyed, he no longer felt at war with himself, his books, or the people around him, and that was a welcome change from the last few months of turmoil and instability. He even started a late-night study session with Chu, sometimes they'll stay over at his house. At other times, they'll skype. Miriam noticed the change and commented on it.

The day of the exam came and after weeks of preparation and anticipation, the students were finally ready. Viyon arrived at school ten minutes earlier than usual, courtesy of his mom. Chu was a nervous mess and Viyon had to keep reassuring him that it would be fine, that they would ace this exam. Mr. Hart came in a few minutes later to announce the start of the exams, he worked them through the process, and wished them good luck. The exam lasted about an hour. At the end of it, the students were given the rest of the day off to rest and engage in whatever activity they fancied. Mr. Hart informed them that the results will be out by the end of the day and they can check it out for themselves.

Chu phoned Viyon's apartment much later in the evening. He sounded super excited. Viyon had to tell him to calm down and speak slowly so he could understand him.

Chapter Ten

"I passed...! I freaking passed...! I aced it!" Chu shouted. Viyon was genuinely happy for him and told him as much. "Congratulations bro, you did it!"

"Yeah... have you checked yours? You should check yours too and find out."

"I'll do that now."

"Call me when you do, we should celebrate this," Chu said and ended the call.

Viyon took out his mobile phone and went online to check, he put in the necessary credentials and hit the send button. His result came up on the screen, with the scores for each subject, outlined beside it. His total aggregate was boldly written at the bottom left corner. He did not pass the test. Viyon looked at the screen a couple more times to be sure that he was seeing right, the results did not change. It was right there, staring back at him. He tried to understand how this could have happened but came up short. A million thoughts raced through his mind, failing his GED meant he had to re-sit the exam or forfeit a whole year. All the people he had known: Chu, Amanda, Jared, they all get to move on with their lives, while he would be stagnated, trailing behind. He smashed his phone against the wall, let out an angry shout of frustration, then smacked his head against the table. The blackout came immediately and he drowned in it. Miriam found him on the floor, unconscious.

Chapter Eleven

Viyon was fighting consciousness, he kept tossing and turning in bed trying not to wake up, he wished he could sleep for the whole day and never open his eyes because that was the only way he could put off facing the world, the first time he tried to kill himself, he had felt something close to relief when he woke up in the hospital bed alive, he had thought that maybe that was a second chance to make meaning of what was left of his life, but this time around he had woken up in the hospital bed angry that he was still alive, he felt listless, nothing made sense to him anymore but he couldn't put his feelings into words. His mother had tried several times to get him to talk to her but he couldn't find the words to explain how he felt, she had even suggested a shrink but he had refused even though he knew that despite his refusal she would ensure that he started therapy anyway.

After trying out several different positions on the bed in a bid to woo sleep back into his eyes, he decided that it was futile. His body had gotten enough sleep. Viyon got up from the bed with a grunt and dragged his feet into the bathroom to brush his teeth, he thought about taking a shower but the thought of going through the motions of removing his clothes and feeling water on his tired body made him more tired so he just splashed some water on his face and left the bathroom, he was the only one at home, his mother had already left to work very early, these days she was at work even more than when they were still living in the old house with his father. Viyon tried not to think of his father, he didn't even want to think of the man as his father, he felt completely useless, he hated that he couldn't do anything to make his mother feel better, "That good for nothing piece of shit," he muttered under his breath as he walked into the kitchen to search for something to eat. The fridge was empty except for some bread, an apple, an almost empty jar of peanut butter, and a carton of orange juice. He would have to go get some groceries later in the day. His mother always stocked the fridge and pantry, but these days, she was always too distracted. Viyon slathered peanut butter on the bread and poured himself what was left of the Orange juice before throwing the carton in the trash, he carried it all with the apple in between his teeth to the sofa, he was about to turn on the television when he heard a knock on the front door. He wasn't expecting anyone; he thought to himself, "And I will sure as hell like to be alone," as he walked to the door, when he looked into the peephole, he was shocked to see Jared and Amanda standing there waiting for him to open the door, he had been avoiding them since he got suspended and even after he got discharged from the hospital, he expected that by now Amanda would have concluded that he was just another jerk and moved on, he cupped his hands around his mouth to check if his breath was okay after which he raised his armpits to his nose and took a whiff, satisfied that he didn't smell too bad, he opened the door, "Hey guys!" said Viyon, trying not to sound as nervous as he felt, he really wished they hadn't come, "Took you long enough," Jared replied as he and Amanda walked into the apartment. "I see you were having a feast," Jared continued. Viyon knew that Jared was mad at him but was just trying to make light of the situation, he had ignored him for weeks and now he had finally shown up at the house where he couldn't give any more excuses, Viyon was beginning to feel really guilty but at the same time, he felt angry that Jared wouldn't just leave him be. "This house is a mess," said Jared again "and really man, this is a sorry excuse for a breakfast," said Jared looking at his friend, Viyon didn't know what to say so he just started back at Jared until Amanda broke the ensuing Awkward silence and said "Cut him some slack Jared, he is going through a thing," she finished, smiling at Viyon. "Yes, that is why we are here, this is an intervention," Said Jared.

Viyon sat back on the sofa and began to eat, Jared and Amanda exchanged looks with each other, shrugged their shoulders, and joined him on the sofa, Viyon took the remote and turned on the television, the three of them sat that way for a while, flicking through channels without saying a word to one another, Viyon finished his food did the dishes and made the house look less of the "mess" that Jared had remarked on when he came in, when he was done, he went upstairs to take a shower, leaving Amanda and Jared alone in the living room.

"We have to do something," Amanda said as soon as Viyon was out of earshot.

"He is fading before our very eyes, his second suicide attempt failed but you know what they say about third time?"

"What can I do?" asked Jared, as he turned off the TV. "He doesn't seem to want any help."

"He doesn't have to want it, it's obvious that he needs it," Amanda said.

The two of them stared at each other for a while before Amanda spoke again, "You have to talk to him."

"Talking doesn't seem to help much in my experience," replied Jared, as he fiddled with the remote control. "We will just have to try," said Amanda. Some minutes after their exchange, Viyon walked into the sitting room, he sat on the sofa and she could smell the flowery scent of the soap he had used. He seemed calmer and more relaxed than when they first came. "I thought you would have left by now," Viyon said, his face devoid of any expression.

Jared knew that Viyon was not himself, he was talking from a place of pain but when he looked into Amanda's eyes, he saw that she was hurt. "I'll be going now," she said. "Take care of yourself, Viyon." "You came with me, remember?" said Jared in a bid to make her stay. "I'll just take a bus or something," replied Amanda. Jared knew that nothing he could say would stop her from leaving. He also knew that it would be better to talk to Viyon when she wasn't present so he didn't object. As soon as she was gone, Jared looked his friend directly in the eyes and said "You need to stop this man, you need to stop acting like your world has ended when it's obvious to everyone but you that your life is just starting. I know things have been hard and confusing for you, especially since your parent's divorce but you cannot let their mistakes ruin your life, you know. You have to live and make your own mistakes too."

Viyon began to laugh, making Jared wonder if his friend was going crazy. "So, your advice for me is that I continue to live so I can make the same mistakes my parents made?" said Viyon when he was done laughing.

"You know that wasn't what I meant," replied Jared, beginning to get a little bit irritated. "You know what?" continued Jared. "I am tired of you locking yourself in here all day feeling sorry for yourself!" as soon as he said this, he picked up one of the throw pillows on the sofa and began to hit Viyon with it while shouting "Come alive!" several times at the top of his lungs, before long, the two friends were chasing each other around the house with pillows, they continued until they both collapsed on the living room floor panting from exhaustion and laughing at how silly they had been, Viyon felt grateful that Jared hadn't left even though he had been rude, he winced when he realized that Amanda had left because of it, he was sure that he had finally succeeded in chasing her away for good, there was only so much crap that a person could take from another. Jared noticed that his friend's countenance had begun to change again. He asked him what was wrong, fearing that their little exercise had been unable to break him out of his funk.

"I was a jerk to Amanda," Viyon replied.

"You were a bigger jerk to me too, but I guess it doesn't matter since I do not have boobs," Jared said chuckling, "On a serious note," continued Jared, "I think you have at least one more chance with her before she gets completely fed up, she really likes you man and I know you like her too, don't ruin it."

"The very next time I see her, I will apologize to her," Viyon said.

Seeing that his friends' mood was beginning to get somber again, Jared said "I really meant what I said earlier, you are more than your parents' mistakes, I have always told you that you have so much potential in you, you can do whatever it is you want if you would just let yourself see that. You have another chance at GED and I know you will ace it."

"Don't get all Motivational on me now," said Viyon, laughing "but I get it, thanks man," he said stretching out his hands to hug Jared."

"Now, who is touchy-feely?" asked Jared Chuckling.

"Come here before I change my mind," Viyon said, embracing his friend. The two of them stood that way for some seconds before Jared whispered: "This is getting weird."

"Yes, it is," Viyon replied and let go. "Let's clean up this place and go to the store. I need to get some groceries before my mum gets back," said Viyon. The two friends spent the next thirty minutes cleaning the apartment. When they were done, they both got into Jared's car and drove to the store.

"Don't tell me you didn't bring a list," said Jared after they had gotten a cart and Viyon just stood staring. "Who goes to the store to buy groceries without a list?" Jared asked feigning frustration.

"My mum was the one who always bought groceries. I thought I would know what I needed as soon as I walked into the store," replied Viyon, laughing at his lack of foresight.

Jared gave him a look that said "How ignorant can one person be?" then began to walk towards the fresh fruit aisle, "Let's start here, everybody buys fruits," Jared said. As they walked through the store, arguing about what was needed and what wasn't, they didn't realize when they bumped into someone's cart. When they looked up, it was Amanda.

"Sorry, we weren't looking," Jared said, nudging Viyon with his right elbow.

"It's okay, see you in school tomorrow," said Amanda, barely acknowledging Viyon 's presence. "I'm really sorry, Amanda," said Viyon just as she was about to leave, I am sorry for being such a jerk earlier, I was in a bad place but you were just trying to help, I know you don't owe me forgiveness but I really want you to know that I'm sorry."

Amanda stared at Viyon for a few seconds before she said: "Okay, Viyon, but this is the last time I'm making a move, from now on if you want us to exist, you will have to act like it, I gave you my phone number for a reason."

"That's fair," said Viyon, relieved that she wasn't as mad as he had anticipated. Amanda smiled at him and pushed her cart away. It was then that Viyon realized that Jared had slipped away when he and Amanda were talking, he saw him standing further down the aisle looking at jars of milk "I hope you didn't screw it up again," said Jared.

"What do you take me for?" asked Viyon, feigning annoyance.

"You know exactly what I take you for," said Jared, laughing.

When they got back to Viyon 's house his mother had just returned from work, she was standing in front of the fridge staring into the light with a look of disappointment on her face but as soon as she turned and saw them with the grocery bags, her eyes lit up and her face broke into a wide smile. "Thank God!" she exclaimed, I was wondering what we would have for dinner. I completely forgot that the fridge was empty when I left this morning."

"You know you don't have to cook mum, we could order pizza or something," said Viyon. "I know I don't have to, Viyon, but I want to, my cooking is the only thing that has remained the same and I would like to keep it that way," said Miriam, with a sad smile on her face.

"Alright then! We will both help out," said Jared, sensing their moods beginning to change "You don't even know how to cook," said Viyon. "Hence, the word 'help', I already told my mum I'll be sleeping over," replied Jared as the three of them began to laugh.

When they were done with dinner and had finished cleaning the kitchen and doing the dishes, it was time for bed. "I'll drive you to school tomorrow, so we have to wake up really early," said Jared.

"You don't have to do that," Viyon said. "How would you drop me off and still make it in time for school?" "Don't worry about me man, you need all the morale you can get, just prepare yourself for school and training, I don't know if your new coach is half as crazy as Bucky but I'm sure you will train your butt off to catch up on all the training you have missed."

"Arrrggh," groaned Viyon. "I honestly forgot about that."

"You forgot about basketball or about training? You know what, you don't need to answer. I wish you good luck because tomorrow, you will remember." Said Jared, as he got from the sofa and walked into Viyon's room.

Viyon turned off the lights in the living room and walked to his room, he took off his clothes and went into the bathroom to brush his teeth and take a quick shower, he went to bed with a smile on his face, he was grateful for Jared, that night when his head hit the pillow, he didn't wish that he would not wake up the next morning and when they both finally fell asleep, Viyon dreamt of Amanda.

The next morning, Viyon was awake before his mom. He fried some eggs and bacon and poured out some orange juice for himself and Jared then brewed coffee for his mum. When Miriam got ready for work and came out to the sitting room, she was surprised to see Viyon in the kitchen making breakfast "This is new," she said, smiling at him.

"Yes, it is and you should get used to it too," said Viyon, smiling back. "Take a seat mum, have some breakfast," he continued.

As they were eating, Jared came into the kitchen, rubbing his eyes "I thought I smelt something good," he said.

"Yes, Viyon made breakfast," replied Miriam.

"Hmmm," hummed Jared. "Interesting." He said as he sat down to eat.

When they had all eaten and Viyon's mother had kissed him on the cheek and left for work, he went back to his room to prepare for school, Viyon spent some minutes standing in front of his closet unable to decide on what to wear to school on his first day back, he finally settled for a pair of blue jeans, a yellow t-shirt and a red hoodie, he wore his most comfortable shoes which were black Nike air force ones, he took some time to examine himself in the mirror, he was normally never this fastidious about his appearance but today he wanted to look good or at least normal enough not to look the part of the "Depressed suicidal kid whose life was so sad that he tried to kill himself twice," when he was moderately satisfied with what he saw in the mirror he ran a comb through his hair and then went to sit in the living room to wait for Jared to finish preparing.

When they were both ready, the two boys made their way to the elevator and went down to the first floor and out of the apartment complex to where Jared's car was parked.

"Wait man, what's with all the colors," asked Jared, noticing his friend's clothes for the first time and trying not to laugh. "It looks like a rainbow threw up in your closet."

"Show some support Howdy boy" replied Viyon, smirking because of the name he had just called his friend "I'm trying to be bright and shiny and full of light, today, there would be enough pity in that school to last me for the rest of my life, I don't want to contribute any more to it."

"Whatever man," said Jared "just don't start any fires."

When they pulled up into the parking lot, all the nervousness that Viyon had been trying to ignore finally got to him, he wiped his hands on his jeans to stop them from sweating,

"You'll be alright," Jared said when he noticed Viyon's angst. "I will be by your side all the way, your Knight in basic clothes."

"Was that supposed to be funny?" Viyon asked, smiling.

"You asked for support, this is support. Now get out of my car," said Jared.

Viyon thanked his friend and was still laughing when he got out of the car, he saw Chu walking ahead of him and called out to him, relieved that he didn't have to walk alone as he could already feel the stares of the other students drilling holes into his skin.

"How have you been?" Chu asked Viyon "I came to see you at the hospital when I heard what happened, but they sent you weren't receiving visitors."

"Yes, sorry, I was not completely myself," replied Viyon.

"No problem man, I'm just glad you are okay and back to school." When Viyon and Chu walked into the classroom, complete silence fell over all the students, they stared at Viyon like he had bird poop dripping down his face, the silence gradually turned into incessant whispers, and Viyon wished he could disappear or at least that the ground would be kind enough to swallow him whole. "Don't mind them," whispered Chu to Viyon as they walked slowly to their seats.

As Viyon sat in his seat trying with all his might to ignore the stares and whispers, he took some comfort in knowing that at least the obvious bullying and fights would stop, he knew that the school would have taken some precautions to make sure that he wasn't outrightly confronted by any of the students again but he also knew that it wouldn't stop the whispers and the snide remarks and stares. "Why did it have to take death for people to just be kind," thought Viyon to himself. All the courage that he had felt earlier began slowly to seep out of him, but he tried his best to stay calm. He decided that he wouldn't let them get the best of him. When classes were over, Viyon breathed a sigh of relief, carried his bag, and walked to the court for practice, he went to the locker to change into his jersey, he was dreading the stares and whispers but to his surprise, his teammate all clapped their hands when he walked in like he had won a trophy or something. Viyon knew that it must have been the coach's idea but he couldn't help the smile that crept through his lips.

"Is someone having a child there, that I don't know about?" Mr. Hunt hollered from the court "because I don't think getting changed takes that much time."

As soon as the boys heard him, they began to file out of the locker room, taking turns to pat Viyon on his back while muttering words that he couldn't make out but knew to be some kind of encouragement. "drop and give me fifty!" coach Hunt said, as soon as they were all lined up, he wasn't as brutal or harsh as Mr. Bucky, but he sure wasn't nice.

When practice was over and the boys were filling out of the court, Coach Hunt called Viyon aside. "I know you have already heard of it from your teammates but I just want to make it official. There is a game coming up in three weeks, and the representatives of several schools will be present, this is a chance for you to get a scholarship," said Mr. Hunt "I know that you have had a really rough time but I have seen you play and I believe in your abilities and I want you to believe in them too, you have a lot of catching up to do but I'm here whenever you need me."

"Thanks, coach, I'll do my best," replied Viyon.

"Good to hear, welcome back son," said Mr. Hunt, patting Viyon on his right shoulder.

Viyon was surprised to see Jared leaning on the hood, of his car when he came out to the parking lot, he was even more surprised to see Amanda inside the car when he got nearer "did you guys even go to school?" he asked them.

"Of course, we did," answered Jared. "We just decided to leave a little bit earlier."

"How did you manage that," asked Viyon.

"Have you forgotten that nobody refuses the kind kids who want to help their friends out of a hard time?" Amanda said, raising an eyebrow in Viyon's direction.

When they were all in the car, Jared started it and began to drive to Viyon's house.

"So, how was your first day back," asked Amanda from the back seat.

"not as bad as I thought it would be," replied Viyon "all things considered, I could say it was good."

"Great!" replied Amanda. They talked about school and training all the way to Viyon's house. Viyon confided in them about being scared to retake the GED and about the game that was coming up in three weeks, they encouraged him and made him feel better. When they reached the house, Viyon got out and opened the door for Amanda to get out too.

"I just want to ask you something, Jared will wait," Viyon said when he saw the puzzled look on her face. They walked to the front of the apartment complex as Viyon tried to muster the courage.

"Would you like to go for dinner, sometimes?" he asked.

"I see you took my threat in good faith," Amanda said, laughing "of course I would, will Saturday be good?" she asked.

"Yes, Saturday is fine" replied Viyon, "I'll be looking forward to it. Let's meet at the restaurant where I used to work."

"Okay, see you then," said Amanda, walking back to the car with a smile on her face.

Viyon spent the rest of the week going to school and then to practice and back home to study for the GED, he was looking forward to Saturday to the point where he became anxious, he wasn't sure what to do on a date, he had never been on one. When Saturday finally came, he called Amanda in the morning to confirm that they were still on after which he called Jared who was going to be on the night shift that day, to remind him that he needed a ride. When evening finally came, Viyon dressed in a button-down white shirt and black slacks, he wore the only dress shoes he had; a pair of brown double Monk strap shoes that his father bought for him, he hoped that they wouldn't look too worn out in the restaurant light, he sprayed some cologne behind his ears and on his wrist and then went to the sitting room to wait for Jared.

Viyon didn't know when he nodded off, but he came to when he heard a knock on the door and got up to open it, "Have you been knocking for long? I kinda fell asleep," he asked Jared, rubbing his eyes.

"No, I just got here. Who sleeps before a date," Jared asked.

"Someone who spent the whole day studying," replied Viyon. "You know you could have called right? Instead of coming up," Viyon continued. "This isn't eighteen sixty-four."

"Shut up man, I'm just being a good chaperone. Don't make me change my mind."

Viyon and Jared took the elevator down to the first floor and walked to the parking lot.

"Amanda has seen you unwashed and, in your pajamas," said Jared, when he saw Viyon examining himself in one of the car's windows.

"That's why I have a lot to make up for," replied Viyon, getting into the car.

When they got to the restaurant, Viyon chose a seat next to the window and ordered a glass of soda which he slowly sipped while he waited for Amanda, he got more nervous by the minute and started to rethink the date. "Maybe we should have gone to the cinema," he thought to himself. Jared came by to check up on him a couple of times, "You are too early," said Jared when he saw Viyon checking his watch. "She'll be here soon."

Viyon waited for a few more minutes before he heard the restaurant's doors open for the hundredth time that night, he didn't look up because he thought it was just another customer, but after a few seconds, he heard the chair in front of his shift and he looked up to see Amanda smiling at him. He had always known she was beautiful but seeing her dressed in a simple black gown and her hair in a ponytail she looked almost heavenly in the restaurant light. "Hey!" said Viyon when he found his voice back. "Glad you could make it."

"I wouldn't miss it for anything," replied Amanda.

Amanda and Viyon spent the rest of the night exchanging details of each other's lives that they did not previously know, Amanda was planning to study Chemistry at MIT and unlike Viyon, she didn't need a scholarship. When the night was over, Viyon said bye to Jared and left with Amanda in her car. She dropped him off at the apartment complex and then drove home. Viyon didn't take the elevator, he felt giddy so he jogged up the stairs to the seventh floor, he decided that he wouldn't study that night, he would sleep and relieve his date with Amanda in his dreams, he was also too tired to study.

In the following weeks, Viyon continued to study and train until it was time for him to rewrite the GED.

All his hardworking paid off when the results were out and he passed with flying color. When the day of the game finally rolled around, Viyon didn't feel ready. He had been training every day for weeks but he still couldn't chase away the fear that gnawed at his heart.

"Today's the day sons, all your training all your sweat and hard work has led you all to this very moment, outside those doors," said Mr. Hunt pointing to the doors leading to the court. "Are men and women whose thoughts about you will go a long way in defining what the rest of your life will look like. When you go out there, do your very best, don't disappoint me, but most importantly, don't disappoint yourselves!" Mr. Hunt finished.

When Viyon stepped onto the court, his anxiety started to dissipate and once his hands touched the ball, they were nowhere to be found, he played like he had never played before and scored the most goals for his team.

When the game was over, he could still feel the adrenaline pumping through his veins and when he looked at the pews, he saw his mother smiling down at him and it took all of his self-control not to cry. As he started to walk to where his mother was, he was intercepted by an elderly man in an expensive-looking navy blue suit.

"Hello Mr. Aleck, I am Mr. Bernard from MIT," said the man. "You showed quite a lot of promise on the court today and I have no doubt that a lot of schools would be interested in you but I would like you to consider MIT," the man said, fishing for his card in the pocket of his suit and handing it to Viyon."

"Nice to meet you, Mr. Bernard, and yes, I will get in touch with you." Said Viyon as the man turned to leave. Before he left the court, he got three more offers from three different schools after which he ran to meet his mother.

"I'm so glad you came mum," he said when he got to where she was standing in front of her car in the parking lot.

"I'm glad I came too, I am so proud of you" she replied stretching out her hands for a hug" When he embraced her, he whispered into to her ears "I got four offers mum, you don't need to worry. I'm going to college," as soon as he said those words, he felt his mother's tears fall on his shoulders.

Chapter Twelve

"I do not have any college clothes," said Viyon to Jared and Amanda, the day before he was to leave for school at the Massachusetts Institute of Technology.

"What does that even mean?" replied Jared.

"Your clothes are just fine," said Amanda, holding on to Viyon 's left arm and leaning on his shoulder.

"Not you talking after you went shopping!" Said Jared, as he threw a pillow at her but missed.

"My mum made me go, she said I was starting a new life and so I needed new clothes but I personally think that is trash. I just went because I would never have heard the last of it if I didn't," said Amanda.

"Yeah, rich girl problems," said Viyon, exchanging looks with Jared.

The three of them were in Viyon's room helping him pack for school. Viyon and Amanda were both going to study at MIT, he; computer science on a full scholarship and she; Chemistry. They had already gotten an apartment close to the school where they planned to live together for the duration of their stay in college.

Chapter Twelve

Jared was going to one of the colleges in their town, "I have small dreams, Viyon," he had said when Viyon had asked him why he wasn't applying to bigger colleges. "I'm really going to miss you both," he said now when they were done shoving the last of Viyon 's clothes into the big brown leather suitcase on the bed.

"We'll miss you too," replied Amanda.

"And you could visit anytime, you know" Viyon added, rifling his friend's hair in a show of affection. When they were done helping Viyon put away the rest of the things he wasn't taking to school, they decided to drive around the town "one last time," said Viyon as they all got into Jared's car.

"Dude, it's not like you are dying or something, your mother lives here, I live here, it's definitely not the last time," said Jared. "Whatever," Viyon replied, starting the engine. "Let me be dramatic in peace, thank you."

They drove through the town, with the windows down, each of them taking turns to drive while the other two put their heads outside to car windows and screamed into the air, they stopped for milkshakes and burger and when they finally drove back to Viyon's house, it was almost dark. Viyon stretched his head to the back seat to kiss Amanda before getting down from the car so they could drive off. Amanda would be back the next morning with her car to pick him up for the drive to college.

Viyon was excited when he got into the house, his mother was already home, she was sitting on the sofa with one of her legs up on a little stool, putting red nail polish on her toes.

"Hey mom," said Viyon taking off his jacket. "Going somewhere?"

"Yes, as a matter of fact, I have a date," replied Miriam.

"A date? That's interesting," said Viyon, raising his eyebrows.

"I have been seeing someone, one of the residents in the hospital for a while now, at first I didn't think much of it that was why I never said anything about it, but he is a good guy and he is kind to me and that's more than I can say for…" Miriam paused before she could make the comparison, no matter how much she hated or wanted to hate Justin, she couldn't deny the fact that he was still Viyon's father even if he hadn't been much of a father to him from the time he was born.

"Don't worry mum, you can say it, in fact, you should say it. Dad was a jerk, you know it and I know it." Viyon said, he was glad that his mother had met someone who she liked and who liked her back, he had been worried that she would be all alone when he left, and that thought had made his college admission a little less exciting, but now he would leave knowing that his mom would have someone, at least he hoped that she would because there was no telling whether the doctor was any good.

"Don't talk about your father like that," said Miriam even though she knew that the word "jerk" didn't quite encompass all that Justin was, a part of her still remembered the man she had fallen in love with, the lawyer who had walked into the hospital where she worked to get a flu shot but wouldn't stop starting at her like she was the only and most fascinating thing in the world, the man who when she had asked why he was looking at her, not knowing whether to feel embarrassed or angry, had replied as he tucked his shirt into his suit trousers. "If you would let me, I will look at you for the rest of my life." It was scary how much people could change, thought Miriam to herself.

"That man is not my father," said Viyon, thinking of the fact that his father had never called to congratulate him on his scholarship even though he was sure that his mother must have told him.

"Have a nice date," said Viyon to his mum, kissing her on her cheek, he didn't want to let the memory of his father ruin what was supposed to be a good night for him and his mother.

"Thanks, don't wait up for me, there is some apple pie left in the fridge, you can have that for dinner," said Miriam, as Viyon walked to his room. She regretted that she had brought Justin into the conversation, but she shrugged the feeling off, it wasn't her fault that the man couldn't be bothered to be a decent human being and father to his own son. When she was done painting her nails, she went into her room, put on her dress, and went out determined to let nothing ruin her date.

Viyon got to his room, took a quick shower, and brushed his teeth. He took out his phone from the pocket of the pair of black distressed jeans he had worn out, to call Amanda.

"Are you home?" asked Viyon when she picked up after the third ring.

"Yes, just entering into my room now," replied Amanda. "You sound kinda low, are you okay?"

"I am, it's just that my mum said some things that made me begin to think of my dad," replied Viyon.

"Oh, I'm so sorry. You should cheer up, tomorrow you go to college! You have your whole life ahead of you, don't let him ruin it for you," Amanda said.

"I guess you are right," said Viyon, feeling better already.

"You bet I am," replied Amanda, smiling. "You should get some rest; we have a long ride tomorrow.

"You too, good night. I love you," said Viyon. "Night, love you too," replied Amanda.

The next day was a Saturday, Miriam was dressed for work when she knocked on Viyon's door, she wanted to tell him goodbye as she wouldn't be around when it was time for him to leave.

"Good morning mum!" groaned Viyon when he opened the door.

"I wanted to wish you a safe trip, I would say make me proud but you have already made me the proudest mother on earth so I am just going to say be happy and make sure you treat Amanda right," said Miriam.

"Thanks for everything mum, I'll call you every day," replied Viyon, stretching out his arms for a hug, and trying not to shed any tears. When his mother was gone, he went back to bed and set an alarm for eight o'clock before going back to sleep.

Viyon woke up an hour later, to the alarm ringing, he shut it off and walked to the bathroom to get ready, when he was done, he put on some comfortable clothes and carried his bags to the sitting room so that he wouldn't need to go back to his room when Amanda arrived, he stood at the door of his room to take one last look inside before locking the door and putting the key on the dining table, he was just about to sit on the sofa to wait when his phone rang, when he looked to see who was calling, it was Amanda.

"I'm here," she said immediately after he picked up. "coming" replied Viyon, trying to carry all his bags at once. He didn't want to make a second trip.

"You could have called me to help man," said Jared when he saw Viyon struggling with his bags.

"You came," said Viyon, smiling at his friend.

"You thought I would just let you go off to college without my blessing?" asked Jared, helping Viyon put his bags in the trunk of the car. When they were set to go, Viyon and Amanda exchanged hugs with Jared and they promised to call each other every day. Jared waited for them to drive away, waving at the car until they were out of sight before he got into his own car and drove off, he did not stop the tears from falling when they came.

"This should be fun," Amanda said when they were a good distance from Viyon 's house.

"What?" asked Viyon, a little distracted. He was already missing Jared, they had been friends since they were little children and he had never been more than a car ride away from him.

"The trip, it's like going on a road trip so it should be fun," repeated Amanda.

"Yeah," said Viyon.

"You will call him every day and he could visit and you could come back home too whenever you feel like," said Amanda, sensing Viyon's mood.

"I know, but you know that it isn't the same," replied Viyon.

"I know, but you will be alright, we will all be alright. Now cheer up and put on some music!" exclaimed Amanda, she didn't want the ride to be a gloomy one.

"Okay," said Viyon, trying to look brighter.

He connected his phone's Bluetooth to the car stereo and almost immediately, Prince's Purple rain flooded through the speakers. Before long, they were singing along to all the songs on the album and laughing. They stopped three times to get food, use the restroom, and for whichever of them was riding shotgun to take over the driving, it was almost dark when they got to Boston and by the time they got to their apartment, it was already night.

"That was one hell of a ride," said Viyon, stretching his hands and yawning as soon as they got out of the car.

"Yes, it was, but I'm glad it's over. I need a hot bath and a soft bed," replied Amanda, already bringing out their bags from the trunk of the car.

They had to make three trips to get all their things from the car to their apartment, when they were done, they collapsed on the bed. "Let's just lay down for a bit," said Amanda.

"Yeah, I'll get up and take a bath in ten," said Viyon, already closing his eyes, the two of them lay that way, not moving until they drifted off to sleep.

They both woke up the next morning to the rays of the sun shining through the spaces between the window blinds, "Oh no!" said Viyon when he checked his phone and saw that it was off.

"My mum must be out of her mind with worry."

"Mine too," replied Amanda, showing him the blank screen of her phone. They both stood up and plugged in their phones when they had charged a little, Amanda went to the living room to call her parents while Viyon called his mom in the room. "Thank God!" exclaimed Miriam as soon as she picked up the phone.

"I was about to call the police, what happened?" she continued, laughing nervously.

"Sorry, my phone died and I slept off, we got here very late and we were so tired." Replied Viyon. When they were done speaking with their parents, they unpacked their bags, freshened up, and went to the shopping mall to get some groceries. Classes were supposed to start next week so they spent that first week getting to know the city and the campus.

College life was different from anything they had previously known, but to Viyon and Amanda, it was exactly the kind of difference they needed, Viyon didn't feel like he had to be anything other than what he was and the new scenery cleared his head and his mind and also gave him a new perspective to life, he played basketball for the school team and was among the top players in the school and also one of the best students overall.

The four years it took for them to complete their courses went by fast, they grew closer together as the years went by, when the time for graduation came, Viyon graduated among the top three in his class and Amanda wasn't far behind either, when he was called to the stage to receive his certificate, he could hear his mother's screams claps all the way from her seat, Jared stood beside her in a brown suit clapping and smiling too. Amanda's parents were also present. It was a glorious day for all of them. When the graduation ceremony was over Amanda's parents offered to take them all for a celebratory dinner.

"This is an incredible feat," said Mr. Baker; Amanda's father as they all walked out of the large hall where the ceremony was held. "Indeed!" agreed his wife, smiling at their daughter, they were interrupted by a young man who asked to speak with Viyon.

"Congratulations on your graduation," said the man, when they were a good distance from the group, stretching out his hand for a handshake.

"My name is Blake, a representative of the National Basketball Association. I know you are one of the star players of your school. Have you ever considered going pro?" Viyon was taken aback, he had thought about this long and hard as the day of his graduation drew nearer, he had decided at the end that a career in Computer Science and Web Technology was what he really wanted, instead of playing professionally, he already had offers from three of the top I.T firms in the country, but now, seeing that the NBA was interested in him made him begin to question that resolve a little, but the uncertainty didn't last long, he knew the kind of life he wanted for himself, he also knew that being a professional athlete would not cater to those needs.

"I am extremely honored, Mr. Blake...," said Viyon.

"... Just call me Blake," the man interrupted. "Okay!" replied Viyon. "It is such an honor, Blake. All my life I have fashioned my skills after those of players I watched on the television, I had always wanted to be them, but very recently I realized that it isn't the way I want to go," said Viyon.

"I perfectly understand," said Blake. "But just take this, in case you change your mind," Blake continued, handing his card to Viyon. At that moment, Viyon had a sense of déjà vu, he remembered four years ago when he had been giving a card and offered a scholarship to MIT, but the difference between then and now was that he wouldn't be calling back. "Thank you," replied Viyon, taking the card.

"Who was that?" asked Jared when Viyon had walked down to where the cars were parked, Amanda and her parents were having a conversation with Viyon's mother.

"An NBA scout," replied Viyon.

"The NBA? What did you say?" asked Jared, visibly excited.

"I don't want to go pro," replied Viyon.

"Aww man, so you are just going to deny me the opportunity of being friends with the next LeBron James," replied Jared.

"I guess so," Viyon said, laughing "I could still be the next Steve Jobs, you know. Although I would really just like to be me and not the next of anybody else." When they were all ready, they got into their cars and drove off to celebrate.

It was three o'clock in the morning when Viyon woke up, he had been thinking of the best way to propose to Amanda all week, at first he had wanted to do something big and overwhelming then he had thought of making reservations in a fancy restaurant but he knew that Amanda wasn't a fan of fancy proposals so he had settled on just asking her at home which was now a beautiful apartment in one of the best locations in Boston, it was large, airy and had a great view of the city below.

They had moved there as soon as Viyon had gotten a job with one of the best tech companies in the City, he had interviewed at the three firms that had offered him jobs and he had been accepted by all of them so he had chosen the one that best resonated with his views and that was Clonex robotics.

He fiddled with the small box which housed the fifteen-carat diamond ring he had bought to propose to Amanda with, after a while of trying to calm his nerves, he was reasonably settled, he opened the box and took out the ring, leaned over to Amanda's side of the bed and slowly and gently placed it around her finger so as not to wake her up, she wasn't a light sleeper but she didn't sleep too deep either. When he was done, he inspected the ring on her finger for a few seconds before going back to sleep.

Viyon got up before the sun was completely out, to make breakfast, he didn't want to still be in bed when Amanda woke up and saw the ring, he fried eggs, sausages, and bacon, made toast, poured out orange juice, and brewed coffee, he put it all on a tray and added some strawberries to the platter to add a burst of color, he was about to carry it all to the room when he looked up to see Amanda leaning against the door frame of the room, watching him.

"How long have you been standing there," asked Viyon, putting down the large tray of food.

"What is this?" Asked Amanda, ignoring his question and putting her hands up to show him the ring on her finger.

"What do you think it is? Marry me," replied Viyon, moving closer to Amanda.

"Marry me and complete my happiness." Amanda had always known somewhere in her heart that Viyon was the one she wanted to spend the rest of her life with, but seeing it become real, made her weak in the knees and she had to rest her palm on the wall to steady herself.

"Yes, of course, I'll marry you," replied Amanda, stretching out her two hands and wrapping Viyon in a tight loving embrace, the two stayed that way for a while before they separated and went to the kitchen table to eat.

"Who is going to eat all these?" asked Amanda, gesturing at the platter, still smiling.

"I was nervous," replied Viyon as he picked up a piece of strawberry and popped it into his mouth. "And besides, proposals are made for hungry work."

"I see," said Amanda playfully, biting into a crunchy slice of toast. The two of them began to laugh and in their hearts, they wished to stay at that moment and never come out.

Amanda and Viyon got married six months after the proposal, they traveled back home where they rented a moderately sized hall for the wedding, they didn't want too many people in attendance when the wedding ceremony was over, they all moved to Amanda's parents' house for the reception, they danced, ate and drank late into the night. Amanda's parents and Viyon's mum were extremely happy for their children, Miriam was especially thrilled, she had gotten married to the resident who was now an attending at the hospital they had only had a court wedding but she knew what it felt like to tie the knot with someone you loved who truly loved you back.

When most of the guests had left and there were only close family members still around, Viyon pulled Jared from the dance floor to sit down with him.

"You know I could help get you a better job where I work," said Viyon, referring to Jared's teaching job at the college they used to attend.

"Arrggh, I thought we went over this on the phone last week" replied Jared "I do not want a 'better job,' I'm fine with teaching, I love what I do Viyon, stop trying to convince me otherwise."

"Okay, I won't bring it up again," said Viyon, remembering that Jared hadn't pushed when he decided not to go pro.

"Good. Not everybody wants six figures for a salary, I already have you for that," said Viyon, chuckling "and besides, if I had another job, I wouldn't have met the love of my life."

"The love of your life?" repeated Viyon.

"Yes, I've been seeing someone, she teaches the class before mine and I think I want to marry her," replied Jared.

"And you didn't tell me all this while," asked Viyon, throwing a punch in his friend's direction but missing.

"I didn't want to steal your shine," replied Jared, I was supposed to introduce you both today but she couldn't make it, since I plan on visiting you and Amanda soon, I'll try and come with her."

"Good man, I'll be looking forward to it, now let's go dance!" said Viyon, already staggering to the dance floor.

Viyon worked with Clonex robotics for one more year before deciding to quit and start up his own firm, he wanted to create an establishment that would cater to the innovative ideas of young creative minds like his own instead of one that was focused on improving already established ideas, he had saved some money but most of all he had gotten connected with many great potential clients and he was optimistic about the prospects, he had discussed it with Amanda and she had given him her full support. He left the office the night after he put in his resignation letter, with an unusual bounce in his steps, he stopped at their favorite restaurant to get Amanda the seafood that she like so much, when he got into their apartment, he found her sitting on the sofa, staring at the table, he immediately thought that something was wrong, that the universe had finally realized that one person couldn't be this happy, he walked towards her with a sinking feeling in his heart, but when he got closer he saw that she was smiling and that she wasn't staring at the table but the object on top of it, "I want to start up a foundation," said Amanda, as Viyon was still trying to figure out what the object was. "Look! We got our first cheque from a donor," she said picking up the signed cheque and showing it to him. Viyon felt the sensation of something falling into place, like the click of a door that had just been properly shut, he stood still for a few seconds, holding the bag of food in his right hand and his suit draped across his left arm before dropping both items and lifting Amanda up from the sofa, he spun her around so much that when he wanted to put her down, they both fell on the cream-colored rug in the sitting room and the apartment.

Two months later, Amanda quit where she worked to start-up a foundation catering to the needs of students struggling with various mental health issues, using the money from her inheritance, and other donors and sponsors, she and a group of like-minded friends came together to make it possible, they went around speaking to students in different schools, spreading motivation and encouragement to them, they created more channels to help those who needed immediate and personal attention or guidance. It was a huge success, and by the sixth month they were employing therapists and reaching more schools in various cities. By that time, Amanda felt she needed to do one last thing.

"I think you should speak at our next one, and before you refuse, I know you are not a public speaker, but if anyone knows what it feels like to be a teenager struggling to stay afloat in this world, it's you," she told Viyon when he got back from work that day.

Viyon was taking aback, he had been glad and extremely supportive when Amanda had started the foundation, he still thought it was a wonderful and thoughtful thing to do but for a very long time since he left high school, he had shoved that phase of his life in a part of his heart that he didn't want to look into again and speaking about it in a room filled with thousands of people was not something he was looking forward to Doing. He was happy now; his company was blossoming and he was married to a beautiful and wonderful lady. "Hmmm, I will think about it," replied Viyon, not wanting to immediately reject the idea so as not to hurt Amanda's feelings and also to give himself more time to deeply think about it. "Take your time," replied Amanda "I love you baby."

That night, Viyon tossed and turned, unable to fall asleep, images of empty pill bottles and slit wrists hunted his dreams, he still had the scars from his first suicide attempt and whenever he was in the shower, he tried not to look at it, speaking of those buried emotions would make everything real again, he thought. Viyon stood up from the bed and went into the kitchen, he filled a glass with warm milk and sat down to drink it, "I am still that boy," he thought to himself as he slowly sipped the milk. When he had drunk the whole glass, his mind felt clearer, he decided that he would do what Amanda had asked of him, but not just for her but for him and the millions of young boys and girls who were trying to find meaning in life, his words were not a cure for anything but they were true, they were his truth and he was going to share his truth even if it meant that he had to hold his heart in his hand to help one person. Viyon didn't get much sleep that night but when morning came, he felt well-rested and calm, "I'll do it," he said as soon as Amanda opened her eyes "I'll give the speech." "Good choice, thank you," replied Amanda, sitting up to hold his head between her palms. Viyon and Amanda spent the next week preparing for the foundation's annual dinner and for the speech.

When the day of the speech finally came, Viyon was extremely nervous, even more so than when he went for job interviews or played important basketball games in high school and college, his palms were sweating and he could hear his heart beating in his chest, he sat in the car with Amanda for a while trying to calm himself, they had arrived an hour before the program was to start.

"You just have to speak from your heart," said Amanda, trying to help calm him down. "This isn't something you read from books, it is your reality," she continued.

"Okay... okay," said Viyon, opening the car door and getting out "it's just a bunch of teenagers, I can do this."

"Yes, you can," replied Amanda, patting him three times on the back as they walked into the school gymnasium.

After Viyon's microphone had been fitted and tested, his name was announced, followed by the sound of many hands clapping in unison. When he stepped onto the stage and the lights fell on him. He could see himself as a boy again, he didn't need any more inspiration. "I was once you," he started, pointing to a bespectacled boy with rust-colored hair, sitting in front of the stage, "Maybe not exactly you," he continued. "But I once had questions that nobody had the answers to..." Viyon spoke for almost two hours, relieving moments of his life that he didn't even know were still in his memory, he poured out his heart and soul to all the kids in the audience, he couldn't even remember the words he typed out and then memorized days before for this very moment, he just spoke as the new words came to him. When Viyon finished his speech, the entire gymnasium erupted into a cacophony of various emotions, there were shouts and claps and tears, Viyon's included. Before he took a bow and left the stage, he looked up to meet the eyes of his wife and mouthed a silent 'thank you'.

Epilogue

Viyon dropped his suitcase on the center table, and he was extremely fatigued. He had spent the whole time at the foundation, answering questions, giving advice, and basically just meeting and helping people. He didn't realize how many people out there that there was that needed to hear his story and be encouraged. Amanda had mentioned how demanding it would be and he reassured her that he could handle it. He certainly did not have this in mind. It was as if everyone wanted a piece of him: His time, knowledge, etc. by reflex, his hands went to his tie and he pulled it loose, he would have taken it off completely, and pulled off his shoes right there in the sitting room but he has had 'the talk' with Amanda a dozen times over for leaving his things littered around the house, especially the sitting room.

"Hey babe," Amanda came out of the dining room. The dining room was adjoined to the kitchen, which means she had probably been there. She looked gorgeous in the little black dress she was wearing. It was a mix of casual and classic. Viyon wondered why she was dressed that way but decided not to say anything and let her unravel her plans herself.

"Hello beautiful," he replied. "You smell really nice. Is that a new fragrance?"

"Yeah… a friend suggested it to me and I thought it fits the occasion perfectly" she smiled. She was beaming, glowing even; some sort of inner radiance from the inside out. Whatever occasion this was; it was definitely special. Amanda looked like she was going to explode from keeping it in for so long.

"Baby? Do you want to tell me what this is about? I might need to use sunglasses to shut off some of this light radiating from you," she laughed then, a beautiful, soothing sound.

"Definitely, go upstairs, take a shower, and come down for dinner. I'll tell you what it's about then."

Viyon went upstairs to shower and got changed then came down for dinner on record time. Amanda's excited spirit and joy were contagious. Viyon found himself excited too, eager to learn what this was about. Amanda further stretched the torture by keeping calm and quiet throughout the dinner. Viyon finished his dinner promptly and could no longer keep it in, so he asked. "I'm ready, I've showered and I've had dinner. Come on, spill it."

"Dance with me," she stands, pulling him up to his feet along with her. "Awwwwww, come on… that's not fair"

They were a few minutes into the dance when Amanda leaned close to his ears and whispered, "We're pregnant."

Viyon could not contain himself, he was beside himself with joy. He drew her closer and lifted her in his hands. "That's the best news ever darling. I'm going to be a dad!" he kept saying those words over and over. He started as a whisper until gradually, it became a shout. All Amanda could do was stand back and watch him. She had expressed that saying reaction when she found out. It had been the last thing on her mind that morning, she had been feeling a little under the weather some couple of days back and had taken Viyon's advice to go to the hospital and run a test. The lab technician conducts a couple of tests and informed her that the results would be sent to her doctor when it is ready. The last time she expected that morning was a call from her doctor and she certainly had not been expecting the news that accompanied the call.

"Can you drink? I want us to celebrate this news… on second thought, I'll drink and you'll just have water."

"With a dash of lemon or lime…"

"Look at that, you sound like a mom already."

The phone rang in the sitting room and Viyon went to get it, he asked Amanda to sit still and be comfortable. "Hello?… Mom!" he put a hand over the speaker and mouths "it's mom" to Amanda.

"Mom, how are you doing? Perfect timing woman. I was just about to call you."

"Oh really?" Miriam asked. "You sound happy. What's happening?"

"We're expecting. Amanda and I are going to have a baby. I don't know the other details, I just found out myself."

"That's great news honey."

Despite Viyon's profound joy and happiness, he detected the gloom in his mom's voice and asked her about it. "What happened, mom?"

"What do you mean?"

"Come on mom, I can tell something's not right. Go on, spill it."

Miriam paused for a while and drew in a long, slow breath. "I don't mean to ruin the moment, but I just got the news that your dad is dead. Do you remember Roberts, his former associate? I ran into him at the mall today and he gave me the news. I know you two did not really get along well, but I thought you should know."

Viyon was quiet for a long time. Miriam knew he was still there because he would never end a call on her abruptly and she could hear him breathing steadily through the receiver. His facial expression must have given him away because she heard Amanda him if he was okay. He must have nodded his head or whispered because she did not hear his reply.

"Mom?"

"I'm still here...?"

"Where are you, I'm coming over."

"I'm in the house," she sniffed and that was what gave her away. Viyon knew instantly that she had been crying but was acting strong for his sake. He marveled at how she could still possibly love him after all these years, after everything that he had put them through, her especially. He had almost cost her; her career, and her son, the two things she valued most in life. Still, she learns that he is dead and she still manages to feel compassion for him.

Viyon informs Amanda of his father's demise and lets her know that he intends to visit his mom and be beside her while she mourns. Amanda insisted on coming and they both went together. Miriam was in the room when they came in, there was tissue on the bed, and on the floor, clear indicators that she had been crying. Viyon went straight to her and pulled her in his arms. Amanda came closer too and they wrapped her in a tight hug.

Roberts had informed her of the date for the funeral and the location. She decided she needed to be there as a way of paying him her last respect. As a way of supporting his mom, Viyon decided he would attend the funeral too and so did Amanda. He might have hinted that he wanted a quiet funeral as it was a quiet and modest affair with close friends and family. Viyon got introduced to his dad's other family and got the chance to meet his kids. His mom instead left after his dad's body had been lowered to the ground. He walked with her to the car, himself on one side, Amanda on the other. His mom let the waterworks flow when they were in the car and they console her. She used it as an opportunity to allow herself to be nostalgic and remember the days before Viyon was born. She talked about how it was for them as a new couple; how they had felt when she learned she was pregnant, and how she had always known that her boy was a special child. In the end, they all found closure for that chapter of their lives and were ready to move on to the next.

The weeks following that event were long and slow. Miriam was still in mourning and Viyon called every day to make sure she was okay. They'd stop by the house sometimes and spread the evening with her, other times they'd invite her over. Weeks ran into months and they began a countdown to Amanda's delivery date. They both decided not to check the gender of the baby, they wanted it to be a surprise so at the baby shower it was a mixed theme, they hadn't done an ultrasound so they didn't know what the gender of the child was, they bought strollers, car seats and unisex baby clothes and shoes they also called some developers to make sure that their home was baby proof, they prepared a room for Amanda's mother to stay when the baby was born. The expectant parents were both nervous and excited.

Viyon got a call at work late one afternoon when she was on her way to the hospital. She had started having contractions. Viyon called his mom after he ended the call with Amanda to inform her of the situation. He arrived at the hospital ten minutes later but was told to wait outside as the delivery was already in process. The doctor came out shortly after announcing that he had a baby girl. Viyon was at a loss for words to express himself. He went in to see Amanda and the baby after they had been transferred to the room and the joy on her face could not be described in a thousand words. She smiled when he came in and said simply: "She's beautiful, I want to call her Dawn, she signifies a new beginning for us all." Without saying a word, Viyon nodded his head, while using his finger to wipe the tear that ran down his face.